GOOD MORNING COMRADES

Biblioasis International Translation Series

General Editor: Stephen Henighan

I Wrote Stone: The Selected Poetry of Ryszard Kapuściński (Poland)
translated by Diana Kuprel and Marek Kusiba

Good Morning Comrades by Ondjaki (Angola)
translated by Stephen Henighan

ondjaki

GOOD MORNING COMRADES

a novel

Translated from the Portuguese
by Stephen Henighan

BIBLIOASIS

FIRST EDITION
Second Printing, May 2016

Library and Archives Canada Cataloguing in Publication

Ondjaki, 1977-
Good morning comrades / Ondjaki ; translated by Stephen Henighan.

(Biblioasis international translation series)
Translation of Bom dia camaradas.
ISBN 13: 978-1-897231-40-1
ISBN 10: 1-897231-40-7

1. Angola—History—Civil War, 1975-2002—Children—Fiction. 2. Angola—History—Civil War, 1975-2002—Fiction. I. Henighan, Stephen, 1960- II. Title. III. Series.

PQ9929.O53.B6413 2008 869.3'5 C2007-907443-X

Edited by Daniel Wells

A work supported by the Instituto Português do Livro e da Biblioteca

to Comrade António
to all the Cuban comrades

And you, Angola

"Beneath the moist veil of rage, complaints and humiliations,
I sense your presence, a rosy vapour rising and expelling
the nocturnal darkness."

—Carlos Drummond de Andrade

I

"You, nostalgic sadness, make the past live again
You reignite extinct happiness."

—Óscar Ribas, *Culturando as Musas*

"But Comrade António, don't you prefer to live in a free country?"

I liked to ask this question when I came into the kitchen. I'd open the refrigerator and take out the water bottle. Before I could reach for a glass, Comrade António was passing me one. His hands left greasy prints on the sides, but I didn't have the courage to refuse this gesture. I filled the glass, drank one swallow, two, and waited for his reply.

Comrade António breathed. Then he turned off the tap. He cleaned his hands, busied himself with the stove. Then he said: "Son, in the white man's time things weren't like this. . . ."

He smiled. I really wanted to understand that smile. I'd heard incredible stories of bad treatment, bad living conditions, miserable wages and all the rest. But Comrade António liked this sentence in support of the Portuguese and gave me a mysterious smile.

"António, didn't you work for a Portuguese man?"

"Yes." He smiled. "He was a Mr. Manager, a good boss, treated me real good . . ."

"Was that in Bié Province?"

"No. Right here in Luanda. I been here a long time, son. . . . Even way back before you were born, son."

Sitting at the table, I waited for him to say something more. Comrade António was doing the kitchen chores. He was smiling, but he remained silent. Every day he had the same smell. Even when he'd bathed; he always seemed to have those kitchen smells. He took the water bottle, filled it with boiled water and put it back in the fridge.

"But, António, I still want more water . . ."

"No, son, that's enough," he said. "Otherwise there won't be any cold water for lunch and your mother will be upset."

When he was putting away the water bottle and cleaning the counter, Comrade António wanted to do his work without me there. I got in his way as he moved around the kitchen, besides which that space belonged to him alone. He didn't like having people around.

"But António. . . . Don't you think that everybody should be in charge of their own country? What were the Portuguese doing here?"

"Hey, son! Back then the city was clean. . . . It had everything you needed, nothing was missing."

"But, António, don't you see that it didn't have everything? People didn't earn a fair wage. Black people couldn't be managers, for example. . . ."

"But there was always bread in the store, son. The buses worked perfectly." He was just smiling.

"But nobody was free, António. . . . Don't you see that?"

"Nobody was free like what? Sure they were free, they could walk down the street and everything . . ."

"That's not what I mean, António." I got up from my seat. "It wasn't Angolans who were running the country, it was the Portuguese . . . It can't be that way."

Comrade António was just laughing.

He smiled at my words, and seeing me getting worked up, he said: "What a kid!" Then he opened the door to the yard, sought out Comrade João, the driver, with his eyes and told him: "This kid's terrible!" Comrade João smiled, sitting in the shade of the mango tree.

Comrade João was the ministry driver. Since my father worked in the ministry, he also drove the family. Sometimes I took advantage of the lift and got a ride to school with him. He was thin and drank a lot. Once in a while he showed up very early in the morning, already drunk, and nobody wanted to ride with him. Comrade António said that he was used to it, but I was afraid. One day he gave me a ride to school and we started to talk.

"João, did you like it when the Portuguese were here?"

"Like what, son?"

"You know, before independence they were the ones who were in charge here. Did you like that time?"

"People say the country was different. . . . I don't know. . . ."

"Of course it was different, João, but it's different today, too. The comrade president is Angolan, it's Angolans who look after the country, not the Portuguese . . ."

"That's the way it is, son . . ." João liked to laugh too, and afterwards he whistled.

"Did you work with Portuguese people, João?"

"Yes, but I was very young . . . And I was in the bush with the guerrillas as well. . . ."

"Comrade António likes to say really great things about the Portuguese," I said to provoke him.

"Comrade António is older," João said. I didn't understand what he meant.

As we passed some very ugly buildings, I waved to a comrade teacher. João asked me who she was, and I replied: "It's Teacher María, that's the complex where the Cuban teachers live."

He dropped me at the school. My classmates were all laughing because I'd got a lift to school. We gave anybody who got a ride a hard time, so I knew they were going to make fun of me. But that wasn't all they were laughing about.

"What is it?" I asked. Murtala was talking about something that had happened the previous afternoon, with Teacher María. "Teacher María, the wife of Comrade Teacher Ángel?"

"Yes, that one," Helder said, laughing. "Then this morning, over in the classroom, everybody was making a lot of noise and she tried to give a detention point to Célio and Cláudio . . . Oh! . . . They got up in a hurry to take off and the teacher said. . . ." Helder was laughing so hard he couldn't go on. He was all red. "The teacher said: 'You get down here,' or 'there' or something!"

"Yeah, and after that?" I was starting to laugh too, it was contagious.

"They threw themselves right down on the floor."

We all burst out laughing. Bruno and I liked to joke with the Cuban teachers as well. Since at times they didn't understand Portuguese very well, we took advantage by speaking quickly or talking nonsense.

"But you still don't know the best part." Murtala came up to my side.

"What's that?"

"She started crying and took off home!" Murtala started laughing flat out as well. "She split just because of that."

We had math class with Teacher Ángel. When he came in he was upset. I signalled to Murtala, but we couldn't laugh. Before the class started the comrade teacher said that his wife was very sad because the pupils had been undisciplined, and that a country undergoing reconstruction needed a lot of discipline. He also talked about Comrade Che Guevara, he talked about discipline and about how we had to behave well so that things would go well in our country. As it happened, nobody complained about Célio or Cláudio, otherwise, with this business of the revolution they'd have got a detention point.

At recess Petra went to tell Cláudio that they should apologize to Comrade Teacher María because she was really cool, she was Cuban and she was in Angola to help us. But Cláudio didn't want to hear what Petra was saying, and he told her that he'd just followed the teacher's orders, that she'd told them to "get down here," and so they threw themselves on the floor.

We liked Teacher Ángel. He was very simple, very humorous. The first day of class he saw Cláudio with a watch on his wrist and asked him if the watch belonged to him. Cláudio laughed and said yes. The Comrade Teacher said in Spanish, "Look, I've been working for many years and I still don't have one," and we were really surprised because almost everybody in our year had a watch. The physics teacher was also surprised when he saw so many calculators in the classroom.

But it wasn't just Teacher Ángel and Teacher María. We liked all the Cuban teachers, because with them classes started to be different. The teachers chose two monitors to help with discipline, which we liked at first because it was a sort of secondary responsibility (after that of class delegate), but later we didn't like it very much because to be a monitor "it was essential to help the less capable *compañeros*," as the comrade teachers said to us in Spanish, and you had to know everything about that subject and you couldn't get less than an A. But the worst part of all was that you had to do homework, because the monitor was the one who checked homework at the beginning of the class.

Of course going to the teacher to tell who had done their homework and who hadn't sometimes led to fights at recess. Paulo could tell you how he got taken away to hospital with a bloody nose.

At the end of the day the comrade principal came to talk to us. We liked it when someone came into the classroom because we had to pay attention and do that little song that most of us took advantage of to shout: "Good afternooooon. . . . comraaaaade. . . . principaaaaal!"

Then she told us that we would have a surprise visit from the comrade inspector of the Ministry of Education. She knew it was going to be some day soon and we had to behave well, clean the school, the classroom, the desks, come to school looking "presentable" (I think that's what she said), and the teachers would explain the rest later.

Nobody said anything, we didn't even ask a question. Of course we only stood up when the comrade principal said, "All right, until tomorrow," and that "until tomorrow" wasn't so offhand because it would be different if she said, "Until next week."

So we stood up and said really loudly: “Untiiiiiiil . . . tomorroooooow . . . comraaaaade . . . . principaaaaal!”

and then I saw that, in a country, the government's one thing and the people are another.

If, when I woke up, I remembered the pleasure of an early morning breakfast, I'd wake up in a good mood. Having breakfast early in Luanda – oh yeah! There's a freshness in the air that's almost cold and makes you feel like drinking milk with your coffee and lying in wait for the smell of the morning. Sometimes even when my parents were at the table, we were silent. Maybe we were smelling the morning, I don't know, I don't know.

Comrade António had keys to the house, but sometimes I was on the balcony and I'd see him sitting out there in the greenery. My mother had already told him not to come so early, but it seems as though at times the elders don't sleep much. So he'd stay out on the benches, just sitting there. When he heard movement in the house he'd approach slowly.

"Good morning, son."

"Good morning, Comrade António." I waited for him to close the front door. "You were here very early again, António."

"Yes. . . . I was just sitting out there, son." He was smiling. "Is the lady of the house up?"

Comrade António always asked this question, but I don't know why. He knew that my mother was always the first to wake up. Maybe he didn't expect an answer, but I only figured this out much later.

"Did you come on the bus today, António?"

"No, son, I walked; it's cool at this hour."

"From the Golf neighbourhood all the way here?"

"Twenty minutes, son . . . Twenty minutes . . ."

But it wasn't true. Comrade António liked to say "twenty minutes" for everything. The water just boiled twenty minutes ago, my mother went out twenty minutes ago, lunch would be ready in twenty minutes.

I stayed on the balcony. In the garden there were some slugs which I figured had to be elders because they always woke up early. There were a lot of them. After breakfast, sitting on the balcony like that with the cool breeze, watching the slugs going wherever they were going, made me drowsy again. I even fell asleep.

It was always the sun that woke me. It was totally impossible on my balcony to work out where it was going. My leg was hot and asleep, I had an annoying itch. I scratched. Afterwards I heard António's voice coming from the kitchen.

"Were you callin' me, António?" I went into the kitchen.

"Son, your aunt telephoned, son. . . ."

"What aunt, António?"

"The aunt from Portugal."

"Oh hell, António . . . and you didn't even wake me up . . . I wanted to talk to her."

"She wanted to talk to your father, son." He was smiling.

"So . . . She wanted to talk to my father, but she would've talked to me. . . . And what did she say?"

"She didn't say anything, son. She just told me to tell your father she'd called, looks like she's going to call again around lunch time."

"But what a time to call, António. I didn't hear the phone . . ."

"It wasn't even twenty minutes ago, son."

The smell from the kitchen, the whistle of the pot, Comrade António's movements: everything told me it must be eleven o'clock. I still hadn't done my math and chemistry homework, and we were supposed to eat lunch at twelve-thirty. I decided I wasn't going to take a bath because I had phys. ed. in the afternoon. The bath could wait until evening.

I went upstairs and "did my lessons," as we used to say. My mother had taught me to study the subject first and do the assignment afterwards, but when I didn't have time, I took a quick look at the material and solved the problems right away. Cláudio, Bruno, and especially Murtala, always did their homework like that, and they said it worked. But Petra was always studying. That girl could drive you crazy, the next day she knew the material cold. When we weren't sure about something during a test, we always asked her.

My mother arrived. First she'd go to the kitchen to make sure that lunch was on the way, then she'd hang up the keys on the key-holder, then she'd come upstairs to ask me if I'd done my homework and she would go and have a bath. I might be wrong, but that was what she usually did.

"Was it you who spoke to Aunt Dada?" She kissed me on the cheek, went into the bathroom and turned on the tap. (I knew she'd do that!)

"No, I was doin' my homework . . . It was Comrade António."

"But António said you were on the balcony."

"Yeah, I was doing my homework on the balcony."

"But I've already told you kids that when the phone rings it's your job to answer it. Don't make Comrade António leave the kitchen to answer the phone." The tone of her voice had changed.

"But he did it so quickly, Mum, I didn't even have time . . ." She went into the bathroom. The sound of the water interrupted our conversation. So much the better.

The telephone rang. I ran to answer it, convinced that it was Aunt Dada. I didn't know her, but I'd spoken to her on the phone many times, which was kind of funny because I only knew her voice. Once she had passed me over to her son, and my sisters and I spent the whole afternoon laughing at the way he talked. I was hardly even able to reply, I almost fell on the floor from laughing so hard, until my mother finally had to say that I was in the bathroom suffering from colic. My aunt didn't make me want to laugh so much because she spoke very slowly, she had what the elders – and Cláudio could never hear me say this – called a "sweet voice."

But it wasn't my aunt on the telephone. It was Paula from the National Radio station, and she wanted to speak to my mother. I said she was in the bathroom, but she decided to wait. Paula was another person who had a sweet voice, I really liked listening to her voice on the radio, but I was frightened the first time I saw her because I thought someone with a voice like hers would be tiny, and she was tall. When I heard my mother say, "Yes, I'll ask him if he wants to. . . . ," I suspected it was something to do with me.

"Look, Paula's going to do a program tomorrow about May Day and she wants to collect testimonies from Young Pioneers. Do you want to go?"

"'Testimonies' means going there and talking?" I said, even though I knew what the word meant.

"Yes, you prepare something and tomorrow she'll come and get you and the two of you'll make a recording."

"But it's for a program?"

"More or less. I think it's going to run on the news, it's a message from the children to the workers."

"So do I have to write an essay, Mum? Aw, that's a lot of work."

"No, you don't have to write an essay because they're not going to let you read an essay, only a few words. . . ."

"Can you help me?"

"Not with the writing, son. . . . You write what you want. I can correct the mistakes, but the text has to be your own work."

"Okay. I want to go to the National Radio studio. Maybe she'll let me see all their equipment."

"Yes, maybe, you'll have to ask her."

It was already lunch time. My sisters arrived from school and my father arrived, too. The house got really noisy, plus the noise of the radio in the living room so we could hear the news, plus Comrade António's radio in the kitchen, plus my younger sister who wanted to talk about everything that had happened at school that morning. She knew she had to hurry because at the stroke of one she would have to end her story to let my parents listen to the news.

We were kind of bored with the news because it was always the same thing: first, news of the war, which was almost always the same, unless there had been some important battle or UNITA[1] had blown up some pylons. That always got a laugh because everyone at the table was saying that the UNITA leader, Savimbi, was the "Robin Hood of the pylons." Afterwards there was always a government minister, or someone from the political bureau, who said a few more things. Then came the intermission and the publicity for the FAPLAs.[2] Oh yeah, that's right, sometimes they talked about the situation in South Africa, where the African National Congress was. Anyway, these were names that you started to pick up over the years. Also, you could learn a lot because, for example, on the subject of the ANC, my father explained to us who Comrade Nelson Mandela was, and I found out that there was a country named South Africa where black people had to go to their houses when a bell rang at six o'clock in the evening, that they couldn't ride the bus with other people who weren't also black, and I was amazed when my father told me that this Comrade Nelson Mandela had been a prisoner for I don't know how many years. That was how I came to understand that the South Africans were our enemies, and that the fact that we were fighting against the South Africans meant that we were fighting against "some" South Africans because for sure those black people who had a special bus just for them weren't our enemies. Then, also, I saw that, in a country, the government's one thing and the people are another.

---

1 UNITA: National Union for the Total Independence of Angola. Dissident independence movement which, supported for many years by South Africa and the United States, waged war against the Angolan government.

2 FAPLA: People's Armed Forces for the Liberation of Angola. The military wing of the governing MPLA (People's Movement for the Liberation of Angola).

After the news, and these conversations, came the sports. But here, too, it was always Petro or D'Agosto who won; well, later Taag improved a little wee bit, they even beat another team 11 to 1 – poor saps! – and the next day Cláudio made fun of Murtala. I think Murtala even cried. At one-twenty, when my parents were drinking their coffee, they turned off the radio. The telephone rang and this time I was certain it was Aunt Dada.

My father spoke with her first, making note of the flight and her arrival time. Then she spoke with each of us, first with my mother, then with my sister, and I saw that she was asking whether we wanted anything. My father motioned to me not to ask for anything big because I was always asking for too many coloured pencils, or notepads, and, on top of that, for a ton of chocolate. I had time to think and I saw that each person was asking for just one thing.

"Are you well, my darling? . . ." Her voice was sweet, sweet.

"Yeah, aunty . . . Look, when are you coming?"

"I arrive tomorrow, didn't you know?"

"No, I didn't know. . . . That's great. So you want to ask me what I want, right?"

"Yes, son, tell me." She must have been really smiling.

"Well, since I can only ask for one thing. . . ." I turned around and nobody heard what I asked for.

After lunch the "lucky devils" – as my mother said – went to take a siesta. She and I had classes in the afternoon, she because she was a teacher and I because I was a pupil. Sometimes she gave me a lift. I sat in the front, put the car in neutral and turned the key in the ignition. Since I couldn't do anything else, I sat there imagining what it would be like when I was able to drive – wow! I'd rip along like anything. Whenever I thought this I accelerated a little to hear the noise of the engine and to give my imagination a hand. If my mother heard, I'd say: "The car needs to warm up . . ." A pretty useless excuse because at two in the afternoon in Luanda a car's only cold if it's got a load of ice on top of it. "Move over," my mother said, as she sat down in the driver's seat.

Later, as we were driving: "Mum?"

"Yes?"

"Is Aunt Dada going to bring presents for everyone?" I asked in disbelief.

"If she can she will . . ."

"But how many people are there in her family?"

"Her and the three children. Why?"

"How's she going to bring presents for us, when there are five of us, and she also asked what Comrade António wanted? . . . Does her ration card give her the right to that much stuff?"

But we were already at the corner where I got out, and she didn't have time to answer. She gave me a kiss on the cheek and told me to think about what I was going to say on National Radio on May Day because the recording session was tomorrow.

It was really hot. Some of my classmates stank, which was normal for people who'd come to school on foot. We stood talking outside the classroom, hoping that the teacher wouldn't show up. It was incredible how we always wanted to believe that we might get a free period every day, because if it depended on us, that was what we wanted. As Teacher Sara said: "It seems that you don't know that your duty is to study." Perhaps that was where we got the saying that the pen was a Young Pioneer's weapon. Or she'd say: "Don't forget that the school is your second home." But it was dangerous to say that to Murtala because he might feel so much at home that he'd doze off in the classroom with the excuse that he thought it was his bedroom.

The talk was good. Bruno said, with that face that only he knew how to make and that everybody believed, that there was a group of muggers who were attacking schools. I'd already heard something like this, but I'd thought it was the schools that were farther away, out by the Golf neighbourhood. But Bruno was always well informed.

"Hey, it's the son of my maid who told me. Yesterday he didn't even go to class, then he came to my house with his mum, and he had these awesome wounds. . . ."

"And so?" somebody said.

"Yo, it was for real, man, like there were forty of them . . ."

"Forty!?" Cláudio figured this was an exaggeration. Even the Zúa Gang didn't have that many guys with them when they carried out a raid.

"The Zúa Gang? The Zúas??!" Bruno continued with that face that was serious only once in a while. "The Zúas are a joke stacked up against Empty Crate. . . . Look, these guys come in a truck, all dressed in black. They surround the school and wait for the pupils to come out. The people who come out get grabbed right there . . . And if you get grabbed. . . ."

"Huh . . . What happens?" Murtala was frightened, his rat-like eyes gleaming.

"What happens? Everything happens: they steal the backpacks, they cut you, they rape the girls and everything. They're heavy duty, not even the police go near them, yeah, they're afraid, too . . ."

When the class started all the guys were thinking about Empty Crate. Everyone was working out his escape route. For sure Cláudio was going to start to bring his switchblade, Murtala, who was a runner, was going to be in the clear, I was going to be trapped if my glasses fell off when I started running, Bruno too; as for the girls – poor little things! Poor little Romina, as soon as she heard the story, was going to start crying and ask her mother if she could stay home from school for the week; Petra would be afraid too, but she would always worry more about classes. I looked at Bruno: sitting at his desk, he looked restless, sweating and gearing himself up for something. At first I thought he was drawing, but then I smelled the glue. Before the end of class he asked Petra for the felt-tipped pens. It was terrifying: he'd made a black-painted crate with a ghoulish skull and had written in blood-red letters: *Empty Crate Was Here!*

In the second hour Teacher Sara explained that the comrade inspector was going to make his surprise visit in the next few days, that they didn't know exactly when but it would be very soon. She explained everything to us again, how we were supposed to address him, how we weren't supposed to make noise. She even asked us to come in with our hair combed. Of course this was mainly aimed at Gerson and Bruno, who never combed their hair (Bruno told me he'd combed his hair for the last time when he was seven years old, but I think this was a fib), and hardly ever bathed, which had to be true because they really smelled, to the point where nobody wanted to sit with them.

Later Teacher Sara bawled out Petra for asking "indiscreet questions." What happened was that Petra wanted to ask, and even did ask, how it was that the visit of the comrade inspector was going to be a surprise if we already knew he was coming, in spite of not knowing the day, and we already knew the subjects we were going to be asked about and were completely prepared for this surprise.

Petra sometimes did things like this, and afterwards she would be sad because nobody supported her and the teacher had bawled her out. It served her right. If she didn't try to show everyone how clever she was, she might be a little less of a troublemaker.

"But I buy what I want, provided that I have the money. Nobody tells me that I took home too much fish or too little. . . ."
"Nobody? . . . Isn't there even a comrade in the fish market who stamps the cards when you buy fish on Wednesday?"

I woke up early and I felt great. I had two amazing things to do that day: one was going to the airport to meet Aunt Dada, and the other was going on National Radio to read my message to the workers. I thought it would be good to take advantage of some things I'd written in the composition I'd done on the worker-peasant alliance, which had got five stars on the Portuguese test.

I went to open the door for Comrade António, and of course he told me it wasn't necessary because he had keys. I don't know how it was that he didn't see that I did it because I had something to tell him.

"Good morning, Comrade António." I opened the smaller door.

"Good morning, son," he said, reaching for his pocket to see if he was quick enough to open the door with his key before I opened it for him. "You don't have to, son. I've got a key . . ."

"You know what I'm going to do today, António?" I thought he didn't know.

"Sure, son, you're going to the airport to get your aunt."

"And afterwards, where am I going?"

"Then you'll come home, son . . ."

"No, no! I'm going to the National Radio studio!"

"Really? You're going to talk on the radio, son?" He was smiling and closing the front door with his key.

"I'm not sure yet. . . . I'm going and two more kids from other schools. I don't know if they'll play all the messages."

We went into the kitchen. "Did you have breakfast, son?"

But I still wanted to talk about that radio business. I was already imagining the comrade radio host announcing my name, and my classmates might hear it too, and what if my comrade Cuban teachers heard it? Would this be part of the revolution? My head was spinning from happiness because it was also a day for receiving presents, and I was finally going to meet my sweet-voiced aunt. I just hoped she wasn't too tall.

"Eat slowly, son, that's bad for you."

But how was I supposed to eat slowly when Paula might arrive at any moment and I had to be ready to go to Angolan National Radio?

I was speechless. When we got to the entrance, a comrade asked my name and made a note on a sheet and gave me a badge I had to clip to my shirt, like I was already the comrade director of the National Radio station. I really liked that kind of badge – wow, just look at the name tag, it was to die for! There was a water fountain in the entrance and there were even two live turtles taking a stroll. I asked Paula how come they stayed there all by themselves without anybody looking after them.

"Without anybody looking after them? What do you mean?" She didn't understand.

"Yes, doesn't anybody take off with those turtles?"

Paula laughed, but she laughed because she didn't know Murtala, who had the trick of taking off with stuff without making a sound, even with animals. Once when we went to the zoo Cláudio bet him that he couldn't steal anything from the garden and when Murtala saw those tiny little monkeys he decided to grab one. The monkey gave him a scratch on the lip that drew blood. Cláudio started to laugh like crazy, but when we got back to school we found out that was just a trick of Murtala's, the dude had wanted to rip off the monkey's snacks. He started to laugh at us on the bus when we were starving and he was scarfing those hard almonds. Poor dumb Murtala, the next day it was our turn to laugh at him, when he had one of those diarrheas that Bruno called "an every-five diarrhea," by which he meant every five minutes.

Paula said we had to keep walking. We went down a really clean hallway. I was stunned, wow, were there really spots this pretty in Luanda? That's the truth, the National Radio station is pretty. I was charmed. There were little interior gardens. I even wanted to ask Paula if I could play there after the recording session, while I waited for my parents. The studio was small and there was a gadget on the wall that looked like a cork in a wine bottle; it was terrific. The other two pioneers and I were lucky because they explained everything to us: how things worked, they even let us joke around and make a few mock recordings. Then the light went out and we waited for a long time for the generator to start up. To entertain us, Paula made a joke that in my opinion was a little dangerous: she said that if we wanted to, we could talk nonsense for five minutes. At first everyone was silent, then she said she meant it, that we could say what we liked. I asked if she was going to tell our parents and she promised not to. But of course the elders never know well what we know and when we started with a barrage of jokes it only lasted for a minute because there were thirty seconds of a triple fusillade and another thirty of her trying to quiet us down. I thought I was well trained. In twenty-two seconds I was able to say all the dirty jokes I knew, even the worst ones, and I took advantage of the other eight seconds to mix and combine those I knew with those I'd just heard, but to tell the truth those other kids were good, too.

The light returned before the generator could start. Then we hurried to record the messages before the light could go out again. When I took out my piece of paper with the things I'd written, Paula told me it wasn't necessary because we already had, "the editorial sheet, with a script for each of you." This made it even easier because it was all typed out and everything.

When we finished recording, we went out into the yard. For a while we exchanged jokes and made fun of each other. Those kids couldn't match my funny stories, but they had ways of making fun of you that could reduce you to tears. Unlike the things kids said to make fun of each other at my school, these expressions were very short, very simple, but very powerful. It was with them that I learned insults like: you swallowed a tickle, you belch when you laugh, the first person to wake up in your house is the one who puts on the underpants, you started going because you drank battery fluid, or the very famous, you took two turns with the chamber pot and yelled, "Angola is great!" They also knew tons of mugging stories. I was about to ask about Empty Crate, but Paula came to tell me that my parents were waiting for me.

"Did you behave properly?" my mother asked.

"Yes, we all behaved properly. The other kids were really cool." I opened the car window and stuck my head out. It was hot.

"How did it go? Did you read your message?"

"It turned out it wasn't necessary, Mum."

"No?"

"No, they had a piece of paper there in the station, with an official stamp and everything. They already had a message for each of us. I read one and the others read the other two."

There were a lot of people outside the airport. It was always like that when an international flight arrived. Next to the door where the passengers came out there was an uproar. I saw the FAPLAs come running. I thought they were going to shoot. I got up on the hood of the car and peeped over the shoulders of the people in front of me.

It was very hot, and I remember inhaling once again that all-encompassing stench. That kind of the smell often told me, too, what time of day it was. . . . But that muffled heat mixed with the smell of dry fish meant that for sure a national flight had arrived. I didn't go to the airport very often, but there were things that everyone knew, or better yet, smelled. I pretended to be wiping the sweat from my brow with the sleeve of my T-shirt and took advantage of the gesture to smell my armpit. Well, it could be worse, I thought.

I got up on the hood of the car and peeped over the people's heads. I smiled: a pretty little monkey was hopping up and down on the shoulder of a foreign lady while a gentleman, probably her husband, took photographs of her. The monkey was going wild, bouncing wickedly on the lady's head, pretending to pick lice off her. Her husband – I guess it was her husband – was a very white man but now he was very red with laughter. Suddenly a FAPLA came up from behind and gave the monkey a slap. The poor sap jumped, did a couple of somersaults in the air, yelled, fell to the ground and took off running.

I couldn't see the monkey any more. A disturbance started. The other FAPLA stepped up next to the lady's husband and grabbed the camera from his hands. I could more or less hear the conversation. The gentleman was trying to speak Portuguese; the FAPLA was annoyed. He opened the camera with a jerk, pulled out the roll of film and threw it away. I think that was when the lady started to cry. They saw this was serious. What idiots, they should have known that in Luanda you can't take photographs wherever you like.

The FAPLA said: "This camera is confiscated for reasons of state security!" Then he explained to them that they couldn't take photographs at the airport. The man said he was only photographing the monkey and his wife, but the FAPLA got angry and said that the monkey and his wife were at the airport and you never knew where those photographs were going to end up. I got down off the hood. At least there wasn't any shooting, I thought, because sometimes stray bullets killed people. Comrade António had told me many times that this happened down in the Golf neighbourhood. "Mainly on the weekend, son." There were people who got drunk, and fired off shots in the air. A neighbour of his had even died because she was sleeping on the mat and a bullet fell on her head. "She never woke up again," Comrade António told me.

Aunt Dada took forever to come out. My armpit was starting to stink and I sure didn't want her to meet me when I was stinky! The wait at the luggage belt always lasted so long, at times bags disappeared and it wasn't worth complaining to anyone. It was just a question of good luck or bad luck, as the elders said. But when she came out and approached us I saw that she was sweating a ton, too, which meant we were even.

She was one of the few older people I'd met who didn't talk to me as if I was a dimwit kid. She greeted me with two kisses on the cheek when I was used to giving the elders a single kiss on the face, and all she said was: "It's very hot, don't you think?"

Now I'll tell you: I was very happy with the fact that she wasn't tall, but what I really liked was hearing her voice live like that, and yes, you could say it was a sweet voice. "Can you help me?" She passed me a bag which I couldn't tear my eyes away from: there was tons of chocolate in it.

As we were walking to the car, I saw that she was looking for something in her handbag. Then she put down the bags and asked me: "Can you call that boy over there so I can take a photo of him with his little monkey?" I glanced over and I felt pleased. The little monkey was already happy again, jumping wickedly on the boy's shoulder, pretending to pick lice off his head, or perhaps doing it for real.

"You can't, Aunt. You can't take photographs of that monkey!" I told her, as I set down the bag containing the chocolates in the seat where I was going to sit.

"I can't take a photograph of that inoffensive little monkey?"

"No, Aunt, you can't . . ."

"And why not?"

"I don't know if you'll understand. . . ."

"Well, tell me," she said, her voice serious.

"You can't take photographs of that monkey. . . . for reasons of state security, Aunt," I said, my voice serious.

But she got the point right away because she looked at the FAPLAs over there, and held onto her camera. She sat down at my side and didn't say a word all the way home. She just looked around, and afterwards she opened the window and it was as if she was doing what I do in the morning, smelling the air.

We found Comrade António at the smaller outer door. He came out laughing, as if he already knew my aunt from somewhere. Of course he was wrapped in the smells of the lunch that I was sure he'd just finished making. I was completely sure, because he wasn't wearing his apron, which meant that he was about to set or had set the table. Now when he set the table it was only "twenty minutes" until lunch was ready.

It was so hot that the first thing we all did was to take off our sandals. Aunt Dada went upstairs to the room where she was going to stay, then she took a bath. She must have been reeling from the heat because she was already starting to turn red. When she came downstairs for lunch, my sisters had come home and they were smelly, too. There's not much you can do in this heat. They went to wash quickly under the armpits before we sat down at the table.

By chance, or in fact not by chance, but because Aunt Dada had arrived and had so much to tell us, we barely heard the news broadcast. I wanted her to tell me what the flight in the airplane had been like, especially the part when the plane accelerates so fast it feels like everything's going to break. My younger sister winked at me because she wanted to see the presents.

Shortly after lunch, because we kept asking, we went to Aunt Dada's room to open her suitcase. It was really heavy and I thought she'd brought us a lot of stuff, but the weight was due to all the food she'd brought, and among that food was my present.

"What's that, Dada?" my mother asked, startled.

"They're potatoes. . . . Your son said that he missed potatoes," she said, picking up the potatoes scattered among the clothing.

We were fortunate that Aunt Dada was very kind and brought with her, in addition to potatoes, a mountain of chocolate.

At times, I mean very rarely, chocolate appeared at home, but three bars each – it was the first time that had happened to me. I thought about the amount of things she had brought. I was thinking that she must have asked different people, each with different ration cards, to buy these presents, but she said she didn't have any sort of card and that it wasn't necessary. As I was late for school, I decided we'd talk about this later.

At school, at that time of day, it was always very hot. People became drowsy. This only annoyed me because instead of telling stories, some classmates slept while waiting for the teachers to arrive. But in the distance I saw Murtala arrive with Comrade Teacher Ángel and his wife. I lost hope that we'd have a spare period.

In the end we even had a pleasant afternoon. We were preparing our lessons the way we would do it if the comrade inspector appeared by surprise, although, as Petra explained to us during recess, "We can't call it a surprise anymore." Cláudio, who always had an answer for everyone, told Petra that it was a surprise that we already knew about it but that didn't mean that the visit wouldn't be a surprise. But nobody paid much attention to the disagreement because we were more worried about Empty Crate, and whether they would appear at our school. Murtala was betting that they would because last week they had been at a school at the foot of the Ajuda-Marido market that was very close to ours. Murtala drew a terrific map in the sand, with Heroines' Square, Kiluanji Street, Kanini Street and our school. It was good that he made that map and explained to us what he thought was going to happen because right next to him Cláudio drew a map of our school and then each of us said what we thought were the best escape routes, depending on whether or not you were wearing a backpack and whether or not you were being chased, and even taking into account the possibility that the comrade Cuban teachers, with all their stories of the revolution, might want to dig a trench and challenge Empty Crate.

After explaining to us the subject matter on which we might be examined, the teachers came with us to direct us in cleaning up. Each class cleaned its classroom, but the front hall and the back yard were divided among five classes, the interior courtyard among three others. The walls were left as they were. Petra said in a voice that sounded as though she was enjoying herself that this visit of the comrade inspector was becoming a lot of work.

As we finished cleaning the school quickly, and everything was more or less presentable, the comrade principal let us leave early, but before leaving we lined up and sang the anthem. Romina invited a few classmates and the comrade teachers to come and have a snack at her house because it was her brother's birthday and he didn't have anybody to invite over so her mother had said that she could bring people from school. When I saw Romina talking to Murtala I figured she was making a mistake because Murtala was always starving and he didn't have the manners to eat at someone else's house.

Romina's mother sent everyone to wash their hands, especially Bruno and Cláudio, who also had to wash their armpits because it was just too much.

The table was very pretty: there were meat rolls, sandwiches, soft drinks, fruit, cake and pie. We were salivating, our eyes so rivetted that we forgot to say happy birthday to the little boy. One person whose eyes were really rivetted was Comrade Teacher Ángel, the guy had never seen so much food in one place. It was fun to watch him attack the jelly rolls.

Since we were making a ruckus, and we couldn't eat any more, because Romina's mother kept bringing out more food, Romina put on a movie for us to watch. I wanted to watch the screen, but I couldn't stop watching the comrade Cuban teachers because their faces, I don't know how to explain it, they resembled my face the first time I saw colour television at Uncle Chico's house – I liked it so much that I spent half an hour listening to the news in African languages. Comrade Teacher María was almost drooling, which she refrained from doing because she still had her mouth full of strawberry compote.

It was a spaghetti Western with Trinità. Everybody was excited, shivering even, applauding and everything, as the actor dodged bullets. Cláudio said: "Hey, I've got an uncle in the FAPLAs who can dodge bullets, too!" But I don't think anybody believed him. Everybody knows that only Trinità can do that. I mean, maybe Bruce Lee knows how to do it, too.

We were all so distracted that nobody noticed that Murtala wasn't watching the movie with us anymore. We started to hear some strange noises, which at first we thought were coming from the film. Romina turned up the sound but it seemed to be coming from somewhere else. Romina turned off the video. Everybody sat still, trying to listen to the silence

The sound was coming from the kitchen.

It made us afraid: we all got up slowly and walked past the table which no longer had any food. Cláudio said: "I warned yuh, Romina. . . ." When we got to the kitchen we saw that the extra plates no longer contained food, either. The two dishes of pudding only had leftover streaks remaining, the pie had been finished off as easy as pie and only two slices were left. But the noise continued and we couldn't figure out where it was coming from. Somebody called: "Murtala. . . . Murtala, where you at?" The sound was pitched a little high to break the silence. Romina's mother put her hand over her mouth and said: "Oh my God!" We all rushed forward to look: we crossed the kitchen and went around to the other side of the fridge. Beneath the tattered yellow jersey, we could see Murtala's huge stomach puffing right out. The dude had got stuck and couldn't get out of his hiding place. Cláudio started to laugh like crazy.

When we dragged back the fridge, Murtala broke free and went to the bathroom where he vomited so much that it was necessary to draw five buckets of water from the bathtub to get rid of the evidence.

Since it was getting dark, the comrade teachers walked Murtala home. Cláudio just said: "Didn't I warn yuh, Romina? You can't say I didn't warn you. . . ."

As I was approaching home, I saw a group of kids around the front door of Bruno Viola's house and I became curious. Before going inside, I went over to see what was going on. I was met with silence. It seemed that the only person who could talk was Eunice.

"There were more than fifty, I'm telling you. . . . More than fifty. . . ." Eunice said through her tears.

"Oh Eunice, come on, you don't have to exaggerate like that," Caducho's brother was saying, but he laughed nervously.

"Hey, whoever wants to believe can believe. . . . The school was completely surrounded. I escaped by sheer luck."

"But what time did this happen?" somebody asked.

"Just a little while ago. We were in the last class and we started to hear the noise of a truck skidding . . ."

"It was Empty Crate?!" I said.

"It was Empty Crate, but the truck was full of men . . ." Eunice wiped her tears. In my head I imagined Murtala's map: Ngola Kanini Street was right next to our school, the next attack could only be on Kiluanji or on Youth-in-Struggle.

"You saw the truck? It was a Ural, right?" Tiny was already filling in the details.

"I didn't see the truck, but some of my classmates saw it. The crate is on the truck . . . it's really a crate, painted black. They arrived, some of them started to jump out of the truck and surround the school, we started to see them out the window, then they began to yell. Four of them who were on top of the truck opened the crate . . ."

"And what was inside?" Bruno Viola asked.

"Nobody could see. . . . I just ran. When I got outside I saw tons of men, at least seventy . . ."

"It was fifty, Eunice, fifty!" Tiny made the gang laugh.

"It was tons anyway! Look, I started running and one of them grabbed me right here." She showed off the scratch. "But I just kept running and luckily he lost his grip . . ."

"The police didn't come?"

"The police?! What do you think? . . . The police are afraid of them. . . . They were all dressed in black, then they stole everyone's backpacks, one girl said she heard a woman teacher shouting inside, she must have been being raped . . ."

"Really raped?" Bruno Viola, excitable as ever, wanted the details.

"Yes, they say they always rape the women teachers, then they cut off their tits and hang them from the blackboard. . . . If there's a tit hanging from the blackboard tomorrow that means they raped her."

Eunice fled, exhausted by her fear.

When I got home my aunt told me that I looked white. It was because I'd been told that they raped the women teachers and killed the male teachers, but nobody knew what they did with the pupils who never returned. At least that was the story that Bruno's maid's daughter always told; it had been told to her by one of her cousins. Now, of course, it was all true, if Eunice herself had seen the truck with the empty crate, and if she had a scratch and everything. . . . That meant that within a few days it would be our school. I had to telephone Cláudio and tell him to bring his switchblade.

My mood improved when I found those chocolates that Aunt Dada had brought, which were so good, so good, so good! that I had to eat the three bars one after the other before anyone could come to tell me that I was only allowed to eat four squares. Then I went to talk with Aunt Dada.

"Aunt, there's something I don't understand. . . ."

"What is it, dear?"

"How were you able to bring so many presents? Was your card good for all that stuff?"

"But what card?" She was pretending not to understand.

"Your ration card. You have a ration card, right?" I asked her this figuring she was going to tell me the truth.

"I don't have any sort of ration card. In Portugal we make our purchases without a card."

"Without a card? But how do they keep track of people? How do they keep track, for example, of the fish you take home?" I didn't even let her respond. "How do they know you didn't take too much fish?"

"But I make the purchases I wish to make, provided that I have the money. Nobody tells me that I took home too much fish or too little . . ."

"Nobody?" I was startled, but not overly so, because I was certain she was lying or joking. "Isn't there even a comrade in the fish market who stamps the cards when you buy fish on Wednesday?"

Later my younger sister came in to ask some questions about mathematics, and I remembered that I had to go and use the telephone to pass along the rumour about Empty Crate. Of course I was already thinking of saying that there were about ninety or a hundred of them, that they'd brought three trucks full of crates and not all the crates were empty, and even that I thought that those crates were where they put the kids who disappeared.

But I was so tired that I fell asleep.

I dreamed, of course, that a Ural truck from Empty Crate arrived at our school, I dreamed that the comrade Cuban teachers showed us how to dig a trench and operate AK-47s, and that when they were about to grab us because we didn't have bullets for our machine guns, Trinità appeared with the police and arrested them all.

The dream was so noisy and chaotic and full of gunshots that my mother had to wake me up when it was almost morning and ask me not to say so much nonsense while I was dreaming.

"But why does this beach belong to the Soviets?"
"I don't know, I really don't know . . . It could be that we have a beach there in the Soviet Union that's only for Angolans!"

I woke up feeling great again because I was going to the beach with Aunt Dada. My sisters had classes and I was the only one who could go with her. This was also great because, as we were going to be alone, I'd have the chance to pull the wool over her eyes without anyone being there to contradict me.

"Good morning, son!" Comrade António said when I was finishing breakfast.

"Good morning, Comrade António, how's it going?" I said, as he was starting to tidy up the glasses, move the plates around, open the fridge and peer inside, then open the kitchen window. He did it all out of habit, it's not that the gestures did any good. I don't know if you've noticed that elders do this a lot.

"You're going on a trip today, son?" he said, and continued moving things around.

"Yes, I'm going to the beach with Aunt Dada. Comrade João's taking us."

"Did your aunt bring presents, son?" He was laughing in a way that meant he was asking if my aunt had brought presents for everyone.

"Haven't you talked to her yet, António?"

"Your aunt was talking to your father, so I didn't talk to her much . . ."

"Hmmm . . ." I smiled. "I bet she brought you some really sharp shoes."

We went out with Comrade João. He didn't turn up drunk because he respected people he didn't know well, and it was rude to make a bad first impression. I mean, I think this was why he was acting this way because he even came out wearing a starched short-sleeved jacket. Maybe the guy wanted my aunt to give him a present, too.

We were driving down António Barroso Street.

"See that, Aunt?" I pointed out the rotunda down below.

"Yes . . ."

"That's the Alvalade neighbourhood swimming pool!"

Comrade João started to laugh because he knew this trick.

"But I don't see any swimming pool, dear. . . ."

"You don't see it because we're far away, but when we get close you're going to feel it."

The car approached the rotunda and had to slow down because of the potholes. There were tons of water pouring over the edge of the road and little kids were taking baths in the potholes and the spot where the water was coming out looked like the illuminated fountain on Luanda Island that never works. The car hiccuped.

"Now you see, eh Aunt?" I was laughing and laughing.

"It's here?"

"Yes, this is swimming pool number two for the Alvalade neighbourhood."

We passed into Maianga Square and I was just praying that the comrade traffic policeman would be there. That comrade deserved to be on a poster: he had a really pretty blue hat, white gloves fit for a wedding, a sash that started at his shoulder, crossed his chest and only ended next to his pistol – yeah, the comrade traffic cop could even take a shot! And he was right there. My aunt didn't say anything, but I saw that she was impressed when she looked at him. I bet that in Portugal they don't have poster-boy comrade signalmen like that.

Afterwards we went uphill and I asked Comrade João to pass by the Josina Machel Hospital, which my aunt thought was called

Maria Pia Hospital. I let out a laugh. I understood that this must have been the name the Portuguese gave the hospital, but, jeez, giving a hospital such a religious name is a put-down. We went down Bishop's Beach where the avenue had just been resurfaced because a little while ago the comrade president had passed through, and since the comrade president always zoomed past, with motorcycle outriders and everything, a lot of people like to have the comrade president drive down their street because the potholes disappear right away, and sometimes they even paint lines on the road.

"Aunt . . . Does Portugal have a moon rocket?"

"No, no it doesn't, dear."

"You see, we have one, and it's not from when the Portuguese were here, don't think that. . . ." I pointed to the left, where we could see the unfinished mausoleum of Angola's first president. "I mean, it's still not ready, but almost. . . ."

When we passed by the corner, Maxando was in the doorway, with his huge beard, his Rasta hairdo, and that face that always made you afraid. I don't know how, because the poor sap was always smiling and spoke decently to Aunt Maria and my grandmother. But we were afraid of him.

"But why are you all afraid of that Maxando?" my aunt said, looking at him as he smiled.

"They say he smokes a lot of weed, Aunt."

"But did he hurt anyone?"

"I don't know, Aunt, but he's also got an alligator at home. That's not normal!" I said.

"An alligator?"

"Yes, he has an alligator in his back yard."

"What? An alligator?"

"Yes, Aunt, an alligator, a really long one. He had a dog, but the dog was run over by a soldier, and since the soldier didn't have a dog to give him, he got him an alligator." This was true, everybody on Bishop's Beach knew it.

"And where does this alligator sleep? Is it locked up?"

"Yeah, it's always locked up. It sleeps right there in the dog house." My aunt didn't seem to believe this.

"My dear, have you actually seen this alligator?"

"I've never seen it, Aunt, but everybody knows he's got an alligator . . . It's just that his alligator only likes to see Maxando. . . . He's the only person who feeds it, you know. . . ."

We passed the fortress and turned onto the Marginal. I saw right away that the whole area was swarming with soldiers, but I thought there must be some meeting up the hill at the presidential palace. On the Marginal there were FAPLAs with machine guns and mortars and suddenly we heard sirens.

"The comrade president must be coming," I warned. Maybe in Portugal it was different and she didn't know. Comrade João pulled the car over to the edge of the road, stopped, turned off the engine, put the car in neutral and got out. I got out of the car as well. Only Aunt Dada didn't get out. In the distance I saw the Mercedes limousines hurtling towards us, and I was worried because Aunt Dada still wasn't getting out of the car. It was too late to turn back, and you could never dash off in front of them in these situations. I spoke to her through the window: "Aunt, Aunt! You have to get out of the car right away."

"Get out of the car? Why? I don't need to pee!" It was amazing, she was still seated and was even starting to laugh.

"This isn't about peeing, Aunt. You have to get out of the car and stand completely still outside. Those black cars belong to the comrade president."

"But it's not necessary, my dear, he's going to pass on the other side."

"Dona Eduarda, please, get out of the car . . ." Comrade João talked like a man in a fever.

"I'm serious, Aunt. Get out of the car right now!" I almost shouted.

It was sunny. My aunt got out of the car, leaving the door open. I felt calmer, even though she didn't look like she was standing at attention. The worst part was that as the cars approached, she put her hand inside the car to get her hat.

"Aunt!" I shouted. "No!"

I think I startled her. She stayed absolutely still. The motorcycle outriders went by, then two cars, then another one, and I think the comrade president was travelling in the last one, with the darkened windows. Later I had to tell her to keep still because we had to wait a moment before we could return to the car. Comrade João was sweating like a pig. We got into the car.

"Oh, my dear, what a circus!"

"So, you avoided seeing the circus of shots that would have happened if some FAPLA had seen you moving around. It looked like you were dancing, then on top of that you were going to put on your hat . . ."

"But do you have to get out of the car and stand at attention whenever the president goes by?" She was completely astonished.

"It's not at attention, but you have to get out of the car so they can see you're not armed or you're not going to try anything. . . ." I'd been sweating, too.

"Oh yes . . . ?"

"Yes, of course. So that's why I was frightened when you started to get your hat, because the cars were too close and they might've thought you were trying to grab something else. . . ."

Comrade João couldn't even whistle. Of course it was possible that nothing would have happened, but it was also possible that almost anything could have happened.

We continued in the direction of the beaches. The sea was choppy, just choppy enough that it had turned that colour where you can't decide if it's green, blue or some other colour.

"What colour is the sea, Aunt?" I wanted to see if she was going to say green or blue because my sisters always saw the sea as blue, they never managed to see the greenness of the sea.

"It's dark . . . it's green . . ." She understood that it was a trick question. "What do you think, João?" But Comrade João just laughed. I already knew he didn't want to take part in the conversation.

"All right, I'm going to tell you a secret, Aunt . . ."

"Tell me, my dear."

"The sea is blue-een!" I laughed and laughed.

We continued to the end of the road, as far as the car could go; we saw the barricades. "What's this?" my aunt asked Comrade João.

"Barracks. . . . It's a barracks," he replied. Soviet soldiers were guarding the entrance. The Soviets always had ugly faces, pale in spite of all the sun they got, and often they looked like lobsters.

"We can stay right here, can't we?" she said.

"No, not here, Aunt . . . We'll go over there by the foot of the rotunda."

"But can't we stay here on this 'blue-een' beach?" She smiled at me.

"No, Aunt, not here. This blue-een beach belongs to the Soviets."

"To the Soviets? This beach belongs to the Angolans!"

"Yes, that's not what I meant to say. . . . It's that only the Soviets can bathe on this beach. You see those soldiers out on the points?"

"Yes, I see them."

"They're guarding the beach while other Soviets bathe there. It's not worth going over there because they're really bad tempered."

"But why does this beach belong to the Soviets?" Now she seemed really startled.

"I don't know, I really don't know . . . It could be that we have a beach there in the Soviet Union that's only for Angolans!"

Comrade João left us on the beach. He would come and pick us up later, in time for lunch. We spread our towels and went to bathe, but I always find the water off Luanda Island a bit cold. Of course my aunt said that it was marvellous. We swam, then went back to our towels.

"Aunt, in Portugal when your comrade president drives by, don't you get out of the car?"

"Well, I've never seen the president drive by, but I guarantee you that nobody gets out of his car. In fact at times we don't even realize that the president is in a car that's passing."

"Hmm! I don't believe that. Doesn't he have police outriders on motorcycles to warn people? Don't they put soldiers on the streets?"

"No, they don't use soldiers. Sometimes, if there's a big entourage, they call in the police to clear the traffic, but it only takes a moment. The president goes past and that's it. Of course the cars get out of the way, it's compulsory there too, but it's because people hear the sirens, you understand?"

"Yes."

"But when, for example, the president goes out on Sunday to a friend's house he doesn't take the police. Sometimes he even walks."

What amazed me was that she was speaking seriously. "Your president walks?" I burst out laughing. "Ho! Wait until I tell that to my classmates! They always want to put down African presidents . . . In Africa, Aunt, a president only goes out in a Mercedes, and it has to be bullet-proof."

We opened the bag of sandwiches. My aunt wasn't very hungry, but after swimming and running I was starving. I ate with pleasure. She warned me not to spoil my appetite for lunch. "Appetite is never absent, Aunt, don't worry," I replied in the manner of an elder. Then Aunt Dada asked me questions about Luanda, what school was like, if I liked the teachers, what we learned, what the Cuban teachers were like, etc. I got a laugh out of her horrified look when I told her that there were a lot of robbers in Luanda, but that it was a dangerous profession.

"A dangerous 'profession,' you say. . . . And why is that?"

"Well, Aunt, it's really risky," I started to explain. "If the robbery goes well and there are no *makas*, it's nothing but profit the next day. But if they catch you, ay! Then your health's at risk!"

"'*Maka*' means problem, right?"

"Yeah, a *maka*'s a problem, a business. It can be a rough *maka* or just a little *maka* . . ."

"And this business of the robbers, what kind of '*maka*' is that?"

"That's what I'm explaining to you. . . . If you get caught, it's a really rough *maka*!"

"Why?"

"Well, Aunt, for example, in Cláudio's neighbourhood they caught a thief. Poor guy, he just liked to swipe lamps, you know. I guess that must have been his business in the Roque Santeiro Market or . . . anyway. . . . They caught the guy, they beat him, they beat him up, they beat him up so much that the next day, Aunt, he came back looking for his ear!"

"His ear?" She scratched hers.

"Yeah, he'd lost his ear there. Cláudio was the one who took him to show him where his ear was because they'd already seen the ear early in the morning, but they stayed away from it because they thought it was a magic charm!"

"Oh my God . . ." She was amazed.

"Wait. . . . I'm going to tell you other stories that are even hotter . . ."

"'Hotter'?"

That was the problem with talking to people from Portugal: there were words they didn't understand. "Yeah, hotter, I mean . . . Look, for example, in the Martal neighbourhood, when they catch a robber he actually thinks he's going to be treated well."

"Why?"

"Because in Martal nobody beats up the robber. Instead, there's a man there, I think he's an elder gentleman, and when he appears the chaos ends. Of course when they catch the robber, right at first, he has to take a few punches, some kicks, but then this gentleman arrives and nobody else touches the robber."

"What do they do then?"

"Just wait, you'll see. . . . Stay tuned for scenes from the next episode."

But she got a strange look on her face. "'Scenes from the next episode'?! How's that?"

"Take it easy, Aunt . . ." I pulled a soft drink out of the bag, opened it and took a gulp. "Then this dude arrives and tells everybody to go back to sleep. A few men go with him, they take the robber out into a yard and right there they give him the injection. And the robber wastes right there."

"The injection? But this 'dude' is a male nurse?"

I couldn't help but laugh. "A male nurse from where, Aunt? What male nurse would that be? The injection they give him contains battery fluid. The guy wastes right there."

"Wastes? What does he waste?"

"Wastes! They waste him, he gets it, he croaks, he kicks the bucket! He dies, Aunt!"

Aunt Dada stopped eating her sandwich. I guess she felt uncomfortable with the story or whatever.

"But is this true, my dear?" I suppose she wanted me to tell her that it wasn't.

"I can even show you a classmate of mine who lives in that neighbourhood, Aunt!"

I picked up her sandwiches and asked her if she wanted them; she didn't, so I ate them! But since she already seemed startled I didn't tell her what they did in the Roque Santeiro Market when they caught robbers. The poor guys, they got tires put around them, then gasoline was poured on the tires and everybody stuck around to watch the man running all over the place asking people to put out his fire. Some people say that when they started burning thieves with tires the number of muggings went down, but I can't be sure of this. Aunt Dada didn't know that in Mozambique they cut off robbers' fingers.

"Cut off all of their fingers?" She wanted to be frightened again.

"No, Aunt, they cut off one each time. One robbery, one finger, get it?"

To lighten up the conversation, I also told her some stories I knew about thieves who got away, like that one on Bishop's Beach who was being chased by the police when somebody yelled, "Stop, thief!" and another policeman thought that policeman was the thief and shot him in the ribs and the robber ran away laughing.

"That means there are lots of different types of robbers. That was a really lucky one."

"Sure, but there are also unlucky ones. . . . Look, in Bruno's building. . . ."

"My dear, does this story end badly, too?"

"No, no, I think you can stand this one." She laughed.

"In Bruno's building a robber was breaking in on the fifth floor, and there was a dude on the sixth floor who takes care of this kind of stuff. They phoned him, he woke up, he jumped down this hole in the floor up there and landed on top of the robber, except that the guy was so frightened he took off running towards the stairs, only, guess what? There was a guard right there waiting for him. . . ."

"And what did he do? You're not going to tell me another 'scenes from the next episode,' are you?"

"No, no, there's no commercial break. . . . He hit the gas, jumped and threw himself off the fifth floor!"

"Did he die?"

"No way! He fell, he played dead, he only waited a couple of seconds, looked around, got up great, he was just limping a little, but when it comes to running, Aunt, I'm telling you: people with limps, cripples, people in wheelchairs, here in Angola they're the ones who whip along the fastest. . . ."

"So he got away, did he?"

"Hey, no way! See what bad luck a guy can have." I thought that expression sounded good. "A police car was going by, they caught him. Bruno said he even felt bad for him – shit, he almost got away. . . . But that's how bad luck comes after people."

By the time Comrade João came to pick us up, the heat had become unbearable. I looked at the trees. The birds were sitting still, not moving; they must have been sweating too. On the other side of the street there were stalls selling dried fish; in this case the stronger the sun, the better the fish. That nice little scent pricked my appetite. There are people who don't like it, but I think that dried fish smells really good, like concentrated sea-juice.

On the way home we passed through Kinaxixi Square because I wanted Aunt Dada to see the tank.

"Aunt, in Portugal do you have a tank looking out over a square like that?"

"No, I don't think so. . . ."

"Well, we do here! This is Kinaxixi Square," I said, by way of introduction.

"But in the old days that tank wasn't up there. You realize that?" She was looking carefully at the tank. She was going to take a photograph but I told her it was better not to because there were a lot of FAPLAs in the street.

"It was a different tank? Was it bigger or smaller?" I hadn't been aware that this was the second tank.

"No, you don't understand. . . ."

"What?"

"There was a statue there."

"A statue? What statue?"

"The statue of Maria da Fonte."[3] She seemed very sure of herself.

---

3 Maria da Fonte: Literally "Maria of the Fountain." Leader of a peasant uprising in Portugal in 1846.

"I don't know, Aunt. . . . Here in Luanda we usually only have fountains, or water that comes out with enough force for a fountain, when some pipe bursts."

Comrade João was laughing.

When we got home they were waiting for us before having lunch. I was so envious: my sisters still had tons of chocolate left. That always happened; I was always the first to finish things.

My aunt went to wash. I don't know why, they say that salt water is good for the skin, so why rush off right away to bathe? In my house everybody's got this obsession with bathing, bathing all the time. I figure it's unnecessary, every two days or so is enough. My sisters say that guys are always like that, they don't like to bathe, but there's a girl in my class who bathes only once a week. That's because the water only comes on once a week in her house. When it does they fill the bathtub and have to make the water last for the whole week.

"Did it go well, dear?" My mother came to kiss me on the cheek.

"Yes, it went well." I gave her a kiss back. "And we saw the comrade president go by on the Marginal."

"Oh. . . ."

"But Aunt Dada almost got shot. . . ."

"Why?" my father asked.

"Well . . . She didn't know she had to get out of the car, then she just about put her hand into the car to get her hat right when the comrade president was going by." I sat down. "She's lucky the FAPLAs didn't see anything."

It was ten to one. My father turned on the radio, but for the moment there was only music. I closed the doors, the windows, I turned on the air conditioning, or the "air additioning," as we called it. I smelled the scent of the food coming from the other room. Without a doubt, it was grilled fish.

"Mum?"

"Yes, dear?"

"Did you know that in Portugal the president walks out into the street without any bodyguards and goes to buy the newspaper?"

"Yes, dear. If security conditions permit it."

"Well, they must permit it on Sunday because Aunt Dada said that the Portuguese president always goes out on Sunday on foot to buy the newspaper. . . . Is that really true, Mum?"

"Is what really true?"

"That he doesn't have soldiers on the street when he leaves home? That he goes out alone. . . . What if people are waiting in line at the spot where he buys his paper?" I started to laugh. "Wouldn't that be funny if he had to stand there waiting?"

We had lunch.

I wanted to know if there had been problems in other schools, if Empty Crate had appeared close to my older sister's school because, according to Murtala's map, I figured her school was next in line. She said no, they'd seen a truck and started to shout, but the teachers didn't let anyone leave the classrooms, and everything was fine because it was just a truck on its way to the barracks. But of course, why hadn't I thought of that, they would never go to my sister's school in the morning. In the morning they'd have to be sleeping, that was why they had gone to Eunice's school in the afternoon, and they had also gone to Mutu-Ya-Kevela School at night.

When I arrived at school, as soon as I saw Romina's face I knew something was up. They were all outside with their backpacks on. Nobody wanted to go into the classroom.

"What is it?" I asked.

"There in the classroom . . ." Romina was almost crying.

"There in the classroom, what?" I was afraid, too.

"There's a message. . . ."

Cláudio and Murtala grabbed me by the arms. Even though I didn't want to go, they pushed me into the classroom. "Look at that!" they said, while they glanced nervously out in the direction of Kiluanji Street. Kiluanji lay close to the way out of the Ajuda-Marido Market, which, according to Murtala, was where they would come from.

"But look where?" I didn't see anything.

"There!" They pointed again.

There were a thousand and one inscriptions on the wall, in felt-tipped pen, chalk, coloured pencil, blood, gouache, everything and then some, and they wanted me to see "there" – but then I recognized the phrase: *Empty Krate wil pass bye here, twoday, at four oclock!* I shuddered.

"But Bruno. . . ." Petra came forward with a theory of her own." That 'twoday' doesn't mean that it will actually be today. Nobody knows how long that's been there!"

"It's today and right now!" Bruno was nervous, too. "If not, how come we've never seen it before? Tell me that, smartypants, have you ever seen it before?"

Petra was silent.

"Well," Cláudio said. "The problem is going to be convincing the teachers that this is true."

"Well it is . . ." Romina didn't have any more fingernails to chew. I warned her that she was about to draw blood.

"They never believe us, but afterwards they're the first ones to run," Cláudio continued. "What are we going to do?"

"By my reckoning we can still arrange for everyone to be absent. . . . If we're all in agreement, no one goes to class," Petra said.

"But it's not so simple, Petra," I said. "Even if we skip the four o'clock class, imagine if they come late, or arrive early, what'll it be like?"

"Yeah, that's true . . ."

"Well, so all we have is a theory . . ."

"And what is it?" Bruno, while looking at the wall, appeared to be searching for the lowest point where he could jump over it.

"We accept that we go to classes, but everybody keeps their backpacks on. . . . If anything happens, it's everyone for himself. . . . I mean, everyone running!"

Romina had tears in her eyes. I felt sorry for her. I was almost certain I knew what she was thinking: sometimes, in dangerous situations, she couldn't move, she just froze up. And she knew that it was going to be like Cláudio said. If something happened, everybody was going to take off running, nobody was going to want to know about the others, that was how it always was. Murtala was so nervous that he wasn't speaking. I didn't even tell them Eunice's story so as not to make the gang more nervous, especially Romina.

In the first period we still took out our notebooks, wrote normally, but we were alert. Those who were seated close to the window, usually Bruno, Filomeno or Nucha, didn't really sit down, they were always peering forward. We saw a truck that everybody found strange and we started to get up. Even Comrade Teacher Sara became afraid. She didn't understand what was going on, but when we were about to open the door Murtala said: "There's no *maka*. That truck's from the Party office." We all took a deep breath, but everybody kept their backpacks on.

Comrade Teacher Sara was really cool. Since she saw that nobody was in the mood to study, she took advantage of the class to explain the details of the next day's parade. But she didn't know a lot about it either. She'd been told at the last minute that our school would take part. She told us only to come in our uniforms, to look clean, not to forget our OPA[4] neck scarves, and that whoever wanted to could carry a canteen. We would gather at the school at seven-thirty, then we would march to May 1st Square. This meant that we would be marching with the workers and with other students, and that we were going to see the comrade president sitting on the podium.

---

4 OPA: Organization of Angolan Pioneers. Government-sponsored movement for boys and girls.

During recess the rumour about Empty Crate spread to other classes. A Zairean teacher in Room 3 packed up his belongings and didn't give a class; according to Murtala, that meant that either he was smart or he knew very well when Empty Crate was coming. The corridors were full, nobody had left their backpacks in the classrooms, and there were even a few people sitting on the walls waiting for a far-off dust cloud that would indicate that the truck was on its way.

Cláudio hadn't brought his switchblade, Murtala had come to school in sandals, which was going to make running more difficult, and Romina and Petra were wearing skirts, which would only make rapes more likely. Nucha had a strap on his glasses, which was good for running, but I, sweating, with my glasses crooked and heavy, knew that mine would fall off while I was running. So I took off the glasses and put them in my pocket. The whole world suddenly lacked definition; but it's not bad, I thought. I focused on a colourful point that was the tree behind the wall that I'd chosen to jump over. Now, I thought, I just have to be fast and not fall when I'm running. Falling was the worst, as everyone knew. When you fall others step on you, nobody stops to take a look, nobody will save you, you get trampled by all those running kids, and if you're conscious, it's the man from Empty Crate you're going to see smiling at you, maybe with a knife in his hand.

"What are you thinking about?" Romina's voice was trembling.

"Ró . . ." I put on my glasses to see her better. "In the next period let's sit together at that desk over by the door. If something happens, we'll take off running . . ."

"That's good, that's good. . . ." She was very nervous. "And where do we run to?"

"You see that stunted tree over there?"

"Yeah, I see it. . . ."

"We run out of the class. If there are a lot of people in the corridor we jump over the wires opposite the classroom, we run towards that corner where the hole in the wall is, and if we can get across the avenue fast, we'll get to the Party office and once we're there nobody'll touch us."

"Good, good . . ."

"The only thing is, we can't fall, Ró, we can't fall . . ."

"And what if we do fall?"

"We can't fall. . . . Take care because the older kids are going to push us. We just have to run towards the wall. . . ." I put away my glasses again.

The comrade chemistry teacher came into the room, and on top of everything else he had put on combat fatigues. This wasn't a good sign because it could enrage the men from Empty Crate. Cláudio gave me a signal, laying his hands on his slacks to catch my attention, but I had already thought about this.

"But. . . . *¿qué pasa*? Nobody has brought their notebooks today?" He began to write the lesson summary on the board.

"It's not that, comrade teacher. Today we're going to have a visit."

"A visit? Is today the surprise visit of the comrade inspector?" He looked down at his worn combat trousers.

"No, comrade teacher," Cláudio said. "It looks like it's another visit." He pointed to the wall.

"Where? Over where?" The teacher squinted to read. "And what is this 'Empty Crate'?"

"It's a problem, comrade teacher. A problem. . . ." Petra had fear in her voice.

"But is this why you are afraid? You are scared to death. . . . But why? *¿Por qué?*"

"They're from Empty Crate, comrade teacher. You've never heard of them?"

"I don' care if they are from an empty crate or a fool crate. . . . This is a school and they will not enter!" He slammed his fist on the desk, but that didn't impress us because this teacher didn't really understand what Empty Crate was.

"They enter all right, and they're even going to enter with a truck . . ."

"I don't want you to sit there with those faces. . . . You're pale with fear! Look, the school is also a site of *resistencia* . . . What do those clowns want?"

"They want everything, comrade teacher. They're going to take some people away with them, they're going to rape the women teachers and I don't know what they do with the men teachers. . . ." Cláudio said all this in a tone of astonishment. But the comrade teacher wasn't afraid.

"Look, I guarantee you that they will do nothing like this. . . . Not here in our school. We will make a trench. If necessary, we will go into *combate* against them. We will defend ourselves with the desks, with sticks and stones. But we will fight to the end!" He slammed his fist on the desk again. He was sweating, sweating.

"But comrade teacher, how are we going to fight against them if they have AK-47s. . . . They have Makarovs . . ."

As the comrade teacher was turning to reply, somebody next to the window shouted: "Oh, ay, Mama!" We all felt the same shiver rise from our feet, pass through the crack in our ass, heat our necks, make our hair stand on end and reach our eyes almost in the form of tears.

Cláudio, before getting up, asked: "But what are you seeing?"

And that classmate replied: "I can't see anything, it's just dust, but it's coming really fast."

It wasn't necessary to say anything more, and if someone had said something it wouldn't have been heard because the shouting started in my classroom, passed through Room 2, and before I had time to take off my glasses the whole school was in an incredible uproar. I'm not even sure if everyone knew why they were shouting.

Romina grabbed my hand in desperation. I thought I'd dislocated my finger bones until I looked at her and saw that she was in a Petra-like state, that's to say, she was petrified, she couldn't move. I glanced at her and said: "Let's go, Ró!" And I thought that we were going to take off and run out of the classroom, but the comrade teacher placed himself in the doorway.

"Nobody leaves!" he shouted, more loudly than all the shouting in the school. "We stay here *hasta la muerte*! We will fight the enemy to the end! We will defend our school!"

As luck would have it, in the midst of the confusion, Isabel got to the front, and she was almost as big as the comrade teacher. Since everybody was pushing, he couldn't hold his ground and was pushed out of the way. He was almost maimed as he hit the grating on the other side of the corridor.

A huge uproar filled the school. It was as though everything was happening in slow motion, but that wasn't it: so many of us were trying to get out the door at once that we were obliged to walk at a measured pace. I remember seeing Luaia's face with her mouth wide open, leaning against the blackboard, trying to retreat in the direction of the window when everyone was moving towards the door. She was always like that: something happened and she had an asthma attack.

It was much worse in the corridor: it was narrow, and the three classes were trying to leave their classrooms, so that only the oldest students succeeded in pushing past the others; they slapped, elbowed and punched to get through in a hurry. Off in the distance I saw Isabel speed up and head towards the hole in the wall I had mentioned to Romina. Others began to run towards the comrade principal's office, as if this was going to help.

Romina shouted at me: "We're going to find Teacher Sara." And she tried to tug me along.

"No, Romina, we can't. That's the first place they'll go, let's just run."

The dust in the schoolyard began to lift and the atmosphere became even stranger.

In the midst of the confusion, I heard the voices of Cláudio, Murtala and Bruno, who was unleashing enormous gulps of nervous laughter. Petra was crying, and there was a backpack that everybody was stepping on, but I don't remember who it belonged to. In the midst of the confusion I tried to add it all up: had the truck already entered the schoolyard? Were they going to lie in wait for us outside and grab us after we jump over the wall? Were they actually going to open fire, or were the weapons just to scare us? Will we be able to run to the wall without falling? In the midst of the confusion, I looked over my shoulder: I could no longer see the comrade chemistry teacher, I could no longer see Luaia or Petra, and I just had to run, run towards the wall.

We got out of the hallway. Now all I had to worry about was not falling in the dust and the people. There was more space than I'd thought, people were jumping over the wall in different places, which was just as well because it was going to be a problem for all of us to get through the hole at the same time.

It was precisely at this moment that one of the most amazing and unbelievable things I'll ever see in my whole life took place: we were running flat out, I didn't run slowly over short distances, it was just that I couldn't run for a very long time because I, too, had asthma; Romina was wearing a skirt, and she, too, was running fast. In fact I think we were both going very fast. Anyway, we expected to be running faster than the person who overtook us. It was the comrade English teacher, a short individual, who, judging by her appearance, had prepared herself for a run because she had her handbag pulled up sideways, and she no longer needed to worry about that; she had her glasses in her left hand and no longer had to worry about those either; her skirt, which must have been long, was tied up at mini-skirt length, which enabled me to see what I'm going to tell you about now, whether you wish to believe it or not: my comrade English teacher, as everyone knew, was a cripple. She had one leg that was more delicate than the other, like a cursory sketch that fails to provide an explanation. But, in the middle of the swirling dust, as Romina and I were running with all our strength, the comrade teacher burst out of nowhere and passed us so quickly that I could only observe those three things (handbag, glasses and skirt). Even so, I only noticed the skirt and the glasses, it was Romina who told me later that she had her handbag tied to her side.

Well, as I was saying, the teacher appeared on our left-hand side, moving very swiftly, staring straight ahead, and with her head twisted a little bit upward (it was Romina who said this), but her secret lay in the way she used her legs to run. My God! I hope I can explain: as soon as her good leg touched the ground at full force, but also with a force that looked as though it was coiling for a jump, the withered leg made two movements in the air, as though it was going to touch the ground but without touching it, so rapidly, so powerfully, that I think I only saw the good leg touch the ground four times before she disappeared on the other side of the wall – Romina and I almost lost the concentration we needed to keep running. This must be a secret technique for running fast in frightening situations, but which I saw because she had pulled her skirt up so high. I'll never forget that weak leg giving two swinging, forward turns while the good leg hit the ground and made her run. People asked me if she was hopping. I don't know how to explain it, I guess she was running, but the truth is that she overtook me, Romina and three other people, jumped the wall without placing her hands on the stone, stretching her good leg to the side and gathering up the withered leg with her arm.

I've seen people run fast when they were being chased by dogs; I've seen crippled people run when they were nervous; I heard about a thief who jumped out of a fifth-floor window; I've been told that there was a little shrimp who used to beat up fat older kids, but one thing is for certain: when Romina and I jumped over the wall the comrade English teacher was already out of sight. We almost got run over crossing Ho Chi Minh Avenue, and since there was still a lot, and I mean really a lot, of shouting coming from the school, we ran without speaking, and only stopped when we got to the National Radio station. Romina was smiling, I guess because Empty Crate hadn't caught us, but I couldn't get out of my mind the image of the teacher running at that speed, passing us and jumping the wall without touching it.

"Fuck!" was the first thing I said. "Can that teacher run!"

Since we were close to my house, I said to Romina that we could go down the street and she could phone her mother. We were already calmer. We met Eunice along the way, she saw we were sweating and asked: "You're leaving school at this time?" I gave her a serious look."What? Don't tell me it was Empty Crate?" She became fearful.

"In the flesh!" I replied.

"How many of them were there?"

"I don't know, I don't have any idea, but everybody was running. We just had time to grab our backpacks and run, too . . ."

"So that's why I saw a crippled woman running full tilt up the street there," Eunice said.

"She's our English teacher," Romina said.

"Hey, and she runs like a gazelle?" Eunice was horrified, too.

"Do you doubt it?" Ró laughed.

I don't know what time it was, but at that hour, from the terrace of my house, you could see the sunset. There wasn't any juice, so we took a bottle of water out on the terrace. We sat there talking for a bit. Romina and I had been friends for a long time, but we never used to talk very much because in school if a guy spends all his time talking to a girl they're going to say that he wants to hitch up with her, that he's sweet-talking her or, what's worse, that he's the kind of guy who just wants to hang around with girls.

"You saw how she was running?" she said.

"I saw, Romina. . . . And I don't think I'd ever seen. . . . If we tell people tomorrow they're going to say we're lying."

"It's possible somebody else saw her."

"No, Romina, not with all that dust. . . . We were the ones who were right behind her. . . . Have you ever seen anyone run that fast?"

"No, I've never seen anything like it . . ."

We sat there, each remembering that moment.

For me it was really good, now that everything was over, to have run together. It was just a thought, of course, but I think that in some way these things remain in people's hearts, and if Romina and I were already good friends, the fact of having fled together from Empty Crate was one more thing that belonged to us alone. We didn't talk about it, but on that day, on that afternoon, with the sun making the moment even more beautiful, I think that we became much better friends than we were before.

"Are you listening to me? Do you think the comrade teacher stayed there?" She gave me a shake.

"Hmm? I don't know. Maybe he stayed there to fight with desks and chalk against Empty Crate's AK-47s. . . . The things those Cuban comrades get up to – "

"You know that they're all soldiers?" she said.

"I know, I know, but a soldier won't last against a truck full of men with AK-47s."

"Yes, but since they're soldiers they're always thinking about fighting. Even so, I think they're brave . . ."

"Sure . . ." I looked at the sun, now almost hidden.

"Just think what it's like to come to a country that's not theirs, to come and give classes that may or may not work out, and then there are the ones who go and fight in the front lines. . . . How many Angolans do you know who went to fight in a Cuban war?"

"I don't know any. . . ."

"I think they're very brave. . . . I never heard a single story about a Cuban fleeing from combat." Romina seemed to be well informed and I didn't want to lag behind her.

"Don't even think about it. On the contrary – everybody knows that they're very brave."

We were told that Romina's mother was downstairs.

I picked up the glasses, the bottle, and we went into the kitchen to wash the glasses, while Romina filled the bottle with boiled water to put in the refrigerator. "This is Comrade António's kitchen, right?" Romina said in order for me to add something. But I didn't feel like adding anything.

"That's right, yeah. . . . Comrade António's kitchen." But her face went still, waiting for something more. "*I'm the one in charge here, little girl.*" I imitated Comrade António's voice, and his almost Charlie Chaplin mannerisms, and she smiled, smiled.

"So, what was that battle like?" asked Romina's mother, who already knew what had happened.

"It was normal," I replied.

"But was there a battle or wasn't there?"

"I dunno. . . . As soon as we heard the shouting, we took off . . ." Romina's mother laughed. "We only stopped when we got to the National Radio station."

"That was some running! I bet you didn't even stop to look before crossing the street," she said.

Only Ró and I laughed.

It was agreed that we would have a snack at Romina's house, where we could all talk about what had happened. In this way we could put all the versions on the table, that of the students and even that of the teachers, because Romina always made a point of inviting the comrade teachers.

That night all we could talk about was Empty Crate. It was amazing, my older sister wasn't the least bit afraid that they would come to her school because they had already come to mine. "You think my school is like yours, right? If they come to our school, my classmates will beat them senseless!" I wasn't sure, she could be right, there were some big guys on Kiluanji Street, people said that some of them packed guns and everything, but even so, Empty Crate was Empty Crate! You only had to look at what they'd done at my school, even a crippled teacher had been forced to run, that just doesn't happen. . . .

It was difficult explaining the whole Empty Crate story to Aunt Dada because since I hadn't actually seen a lot – as a matter of fact I hadn't actually seen anything at all – I couldn't tell her who they were, or what they looked like, or what had happened because, and there it was, all these details would become known only the next day.

Since I was tired and had to wake up early, I went to bed.

"Till tomorrow, everybody!" I said as I left.

at times all the big things in life can be seen in one small thing. You don't have to explain much: it's enough to look.

I woke up feeling great again because I loved rallies and parades.

"Good morning, Comrade Father!" I said jokingly, since Comrade António hadn't yet arrived.

"Good morning, Comrade Son!" he replied, feeling great in the morning as he always did. The milk was already warm, the table had been set the night before. I opened the window wide, and the brightness came in as if it were a stranger entering an unknown spot and looking around out of curiosity.

From my place at the table I saw the cup in front of me, the steam that rose from the cup, and I smelled the toast and the butter melting on it, I saw the right side of my father's beard, his glasses, and I heard the sound in his mouth as he chewed his toast, *crunch, crunch*, but prettiest of all was seeing the avocado tree opposite. Did you know that avocado trees also stretch?

"Dad, have you noticed that in the morning, when we open this window and sit here talking, the avocado tree starts trembling?"

"Yes, son, it trembles in the wind. . . ."

"Yeah, but why doesn't it tremble before we open the window? Now I've got you . . ."

"It's shaking before you open the window, son. It's you who can't see it."

"So it only shakes when I open the window . . . And it doesn't shake, Dad, it's not real shaking . . ."

"What is it, then?" He motioned with his finger for me to start eating my toast.

"It's stretching. . . . The avocado tree is stretching itself." By saying "stretching itself," I was being refined, like the Portuguese, because usually we would just say "stretching."

The light came in through the enormous window, the birds' chirping came in, the sound of the water dripping into the tank came in, the smell of the morning came in, the noise of the boots of the security guards at the house next door came in, the shriek of a tomcat preparing to fight with another tomcat came in, the noise of the larder being opened by my mother came in, the sound of a car horn came in, a fat fly came in, a dragonfly that we called a draggin'-fly came in, the noise of the tomcat which after fighting jumped on the zinc roof came in, the sound of the security guard setting down his AK-47 to take a rest came in, whistling came in, much more light came in, and, above all, the smell of the avocado tree came in, the smell of the avocado tree that was waking up.

"Dad, it's a holiday today. If you're not going to the rally, why didn't you get up later?" I finally bit into the toast.

"Because I like to get up early!" He lit a cigarette.

I put on my backpack and my father got up to open the door for me.

"Good morning, son." I heard the voice coming from the creepers. I was frightened: it was Comrade António!

"Good morning, Comrade António!"

"Did I frighten you, son?" He was laughing.

"António, it's a holiday today. What are you doing here?"

"I came for a walk, son. . . . I wake up early every morning."

"Hey, António . . ." I said, horrified. "Instead of taking advantage of your day off to sleep . . . And today you came on foot, there aren't any buses this early. . . ."

"It's twenty minutes, son, twenty minutes on foot . . ."

"Okay, see you at lunch time," I said as I left.

"Are you going to see the comrade president, son?"

"Yeah, I'm going to the rally on May 1st Square, but we're meeting at school."

"See you later then, son."

"See you later, António."

I stopped by at Bruno Viola's house, but he wasn't ready yet. I left.

Because of all this, I was already late. I wanted to see if I'd be able to chat for a bit with Cláudio or Murtala about the previous day's events. It was possible that they'd seen more than I had. Murtala wasn't to be trusted because he always exaggerated stories. I mean, everybody I know here in Luanda exaggerates, but Murtala, as Petra used to say, was too much. Once they'd caught an alligator on Luanda Island and Murtala said that a whale had run aground in Luanda Bay. If Murtala had seen a soccer match and nobody knew the result, you could be sure that Murtala would add seven goals here, twenty-two penalties there, two expulsions and an injury to the referee. Bruno gave him good advice: "When you want to fib, fib little by little – that way we might believe you!"

I was so late that the classes were already lined up when I arrived. Comrade Teacher Sara saw me arrive and put on her I-am-not-pleased face. We stood in straight lines, in order. They were inspecting the neck-scarves. Anyone who didn't have a neck scarf could go home, this was the May 1st parade, the international day of the worker, and no child without the full dress uniform was allowed to take part. We started to sing: "Oh homeland, we will never forget/ The heroes of the fourth of February . . ." But Cláudio and I were looking for signs. How was it possible for the school to remain so intact (I'd learned this word from Petra) after the attack by Empty Crate? There weren't even tire marks on the ground, there were no bullet holes in the walls, and all the female and male teachers were present, including the chemistry teacher, who was concentrating hard even though he didn't know all the words of the anthem, and the speedy (I think that's the best way to put it) comrade English teacher.

When the anthem ended, the comrade principal explained rapidly that we were going to march to May 1st Square, that she wanted the lines to remain in order and that she didn't want any running (to avoid the smell of sweat), that afterwards we were going to join the general gathering of the schools on the square and that then we would find out our position in the parade. Oh – and if anyone needed to pee they could do so, but that it was too late to take a pooh because we didn't have time now. In any event, nobody ever took a pooh at school because the school didn't have bathrooms. I don't know why she gave us this lecture, using that word, which she shouldn't have spoken in front of a rally.

Romina looked in my direction and gave me a sign with her eyes for me to look at the steps. There she was, the comrade English teacher, limping slowly from side to side. "Who saw you and who sees you now?" Romina said under her breath, and I grasped right away that this saying was directed at me.

Later, when we had already begun to march towards May 1st Square, I noticed that Murtala had a bandage on his ankle. That was a good sign: something had actually happened. He didn't look in my direction, nor in Cláudio's direction. I realized he didn't want to talk, much less to answer questions. When Cláudio tried to talk to him he took a fit and called Comrade Teacher Sara, who bawled out Cláudio. Cláudio responded with a disparaging whistle that could even be heard at the back of the line. Good, I thought; that Murtala was making a fuss about nothing, the idiot.

In the square, a comrade from the Ministry of Education came to hand out little red and yellow flags, some national flags and others of the MPLA. I looked at the podium and thought I made out the comrade president, but we were still far away, you could see only that the podium was full and there were soldiers all around the top, and in the streets, as well. The comrade president probably hadn't arrived yet. Everyone had little flags, the mammies from OMA[5], the young people from "the J,"[6] the pioneers from OPA, the comrade workers, the people who had come to take part: the square was full of colour and movement. The comrade at the microphone was warming people up.

"A single people a single. . . . ?" he said.

". . . NATION!!!" we shouted with all our might. We always took advantage of the opportunity to shout.

"A single people a single . . . ?"

". . . NATION!!!"

"The struggle. . . . ?"

"CONTINUES!!!"

"The struggle. . . . ?"

"CONTINUES!!!"

"But the struggle, comrades?" He was shouting, too. The guy was delighted.

"CONTINUES!!!!!!!!!!!"

"And victory . . . ?"

"IS CERTAIN!!!"

"Victory . . . ?"

"IS CERTAIN!!!"

"The MPLA is the people. . . ."

"AND THE PEOPLE ARE THE MPLA!!!"

"The MPLA is the people. . . ."

"AND THE PEOPLE ARE THE MPLA!!!"

"Down with imperialism . . ."

"DOWN!!!"

"Down with imperialism . . ."

"DOWN!!!"

"Thank you, comrades."

---

5 OMA: Organization of Angolan Women (government-sponsored).

6 JMPLA: Youth of the People's Movement for the Liberation of Angola.

Some kids were already going hoarse, but we loved to shout the slogans. We heard the sirens. The convoy of Mercedes approached in the distance, this time, yes, it was the comrade president. The people were yelling and clapping their hands. "DOS SANTOS.... FRIEND.... THE PEOPLE FOLLOW YOU TO THE END! DOS SANTOS.... FRIEND.... THE PEOPLE FOLLOW YOU TO THE END!"

Only Murtala seemed not to feel like making noise. I approached him and offered him water from my canteen. "You want a little bit?" I pulled off the cap.

"No, I'm not going to drink from your canteen. . . ."

"Why not?" I took a swallow.

"Because you've got asthma."

Once, a long time ago, it had been the other way around: Petra hadn't allowed me to drink from her canteen because of asthma. But Murtala didn't worry about this sort of thing. He must be really pissed off. "Don't expect me to offer it to you again," I snapped.

The schools were starting to line up again, the shortest classes in front, the big kids at the back. "DOS SANTOS.... FRIEND.... THE OPA FOLLOWS YOU TO THE END! DOS SANTOS.... FRIEND.... THE OPA FOLLOWS YOU TO THE END!" That was what we shouted as we walked in front of the comrade president. He was on his feet, clapping his hands and laughing. There were so many people shouting that he couldn't have heard our child-like shouts.

There were so many people that I was afraid. If something happened here, for example, if a bomb went off, or even Empty Crate. . . . a lot of people would be trampled to death by other people, which is the worst way to be trampled. It's true, it's sad, but a person can crush another person.

The journalists were lined up on the right-hand side. They only took photographs now and then – to save film, I think. Some of them were already breaking formation to bring their cameras or television equipment closer. We'd been told that comrades from

Soviet television would also be coming to film the parade. But they must have been very well hidden because I didn't see any Soviets.

Paula was there with a microphone in her hand, a recorder on her shoulder. She was laughing as she ran alongside a comrade teacher. I think she was trying to interview him. "Paula! Paula!" I shouted, but we were too far ahead of her and she didn't hear me. After passing in front of the podium, we walked a little farther and then our school stopped because the comrade principal said that they were going to give us biscuits and juice, but no one came. I guess it must have been because of the lack of cash, because that was why they didn't have floats in this year's parade. Maybe that was why they invited so many schools: to see whether the parade could still look good without floats. But for me, to tell the truth, the May Day parade just wasn't the same without floats. For next year, if they call me to talk on National Radio again, that's exactly what I'm going to say. I don't want to know anything about any sheet of paper with an official stamp and everything already written on it.

Since neither the juice nor the biscuits had appeared, the comrade principal ordered us to demobilize. We were all free to go home. But we had arranged to go to the school and bring our discussion about Empty Crate up to date, and we'd said that even if we didn't see each other along the way, we would meet at the school after the rally.

The girls, as always, arrived together: Petra, Romina and even Luaia. Bruno and I arrived, then Cláudio with tons of biscuits and two bottles of juice. But he refused to give anything to anyone else; he was always such a selfish guy. He said: "Sorry about that, but, as my cousin said, my hunger is in a category by itself!" It must have been a pretty special category because he managed to eat everything without anyone else getting a crumb.

"But Murtala's missing," somebody said.

"He's not comin'," Cláudio warned us, his mouth full.

"What do you mean he's not coming? We arranged to be here. . . ."

"I'm tellin' yuh, he's not comin'. . . . I saw him taking off the other way, up the hill . . ."

"He was weird today. . . . Didn't you think so, Cláudio?" I asked.

"Yeah, a little. . . ."

"He didn't even want a drink of water when I offered him one. . . ."

"Yeah." Cláudio started laughing. "Asthma-water. . . ."

"Hey, you jerk. Have you ever heard water cough?"

"No."

"All right, then don't talk bullshit."

We went to our classroom. Everything was the same. The desks were there, there were no bloodstains, no tits hung from the blackboard. We sat down outside on the low wall that closed off the yard. The air had no smell. Everything was calm even though we could hear, off in the distance, the noise of the rest of the crowd on May 1st Square.

So, what Cláudio said: "I was one of the first to leave the classroom. When Isabel threw the comrade teacher out of the way, I was the only one right behind her. I didn't look to either side or anything. I was terrified of seeing some man with an AK-47 in his hands and becoming petrified with fear. I took off running behind her. I'm telling you, it was the best thing to do because Isabel cut through the crowd like a knife. I saw two little girls fall over after Isabel pushed them out of the way. I kept on going right behind her, I jumped the wall behind her and headed in the direction of May 1st Square. I only stopped when I got to the Atlantic Cinema. I never looked back. I remember hearing the noise of that truck, but I'd already jumped the wall. I figured I was in the clear, and those bastards would never get me. When I stopped to look in the direction of the school, I saw everybody running and shouting, and I decided it was better to go straight home."

What Petra said: "I don't remember how I got out of the room because there was such an uproar I couldn't even think. Everybody was pushing me towards the door and I saw the comrade teacher pushed back against the wire, even though he kept shouting that we had to fight back, that it was useless to run from the enemy, that we must confront him with all the weapons at our disposal. I started to get annoyed when Célio came up from behind. He was pushing everyone, trying to climb over people's shoulders, as if he was in more of a hurry than the rest of us, but I gave him a smack and he got back into the line to run away. I mean, even if you're running away, there's got to be some kind of organization, it can't just be a free-for-all. But I'm telling you, that smack was my salvation because he gave me a push that made me jump over the wall. I don't know if he did it because he was upset or if he was feeling me up, but the truth is that without his help I wouldn't have managed to jump over that wall. I ran towards the Square as well, and that was where I met a comrade policeman. I stood at his feet and I only realized my backpack was ripped open when he asked me if I was crying because of my ripped backpack."

What Bruno said: "I was one of the first to see the truck's dust in the distance, but to tell the truth it wasn't possible to see if it was a Ural or not. I remember that it approached at high speed and that I only had time to shout once because when I tried to shout a second time the whole school was shouting. I grabbed my backpack, I jumped over Filomeno, who I think fell down, and the last thing I saw before leaving the classroom was Luaia's face. She looked like she was drowning, and she was leaning up in the corner, or, possibly it was worse than that because that was where the board brush was shaken out. When I got to the ramp in the schoolyard I wanted to run with all the speed in my legs, but I couldn't help starting to laugh, and it wasn't from fear or nerves: it was because I saw the comrade English teacher lift her skirt as if she was going to have a pee but without ever breaking stride, which doesn't explain how she was able to run, because I didn't see, I wasn't able to see. When she took off she disappeared into the clouds of dust and when I succeeded in getting over the wall she was gone. I crossed Heroines' Square without looking out for cars, and the guy who was behind me, a neighbour of mine, said that I just missed getting run over by a Volkswagen, but I swear I didn't see a thing. I only stopped running when I reached the door of my building and even then my mother boxed my ears because she'd already told me not to go running around all over the place like that because it made me dirty and sweaty. And when I said that it was because of Empty Crate, I got my ears boxed again for lying; I didn't know what to do."

What Luaia said: "I remember very clearly seeing you pass me, Bruno, but it wasn't because I'd fallen in the corner. You were the one who pushed me and I ended up with my nose in the chalk box, where the board brush was as well. But it doesn't matter, I think that right from the first shouts my asthma started, and I decided it was better to stay there, so that while all of you were running, I was lying on the floor. So I can't say that I saw something because I didn't see anything. I heard the shouting outside and I was scared to death because after the shouting the shooting would start, or they would come and get me. I was afraid that they wouldn't find any women teachers and that they'd want to rape me instead. Worst of all, afterwards they would tear my tit off and pin it to the blackboard. But I was so scared and so short of breath that I think I fainted, and when I came to I was already in the comrade principal's office, and Comrade Teacher Sara and the comrade chemistry teacher were there."

What I, Ndalu, said: "I was sitting with Romina and since there was an opening we ran out, also in the middle of the crowd. I was afraid of falling, or afraid that after running and getting over the wall, we'd find that they'd encircled the school outside the wall. I didn't see any truck, or any dust. I think I started running right in the classroom when Bruno shouted for the second time, which may have been the same time that everybody in the school shouted at once. I just want to say one thing, you guys don't have to believe me, but the comrade English teacher, for those of you who didn't see I'm telling you: she could be an Angolan international Olympic champion . . . She passed me and Romina so fast that when I looked she was already jumping the wall, and you'd better believe, I swear on Christ's wounds, and on the soul of my grandfather, may he rest in peace, she jumped the wall without touching it. She just put a leg out to the side and grabbed her crippled leg with her hand and gathered herself up as if she was scratching her thigh, and if you don't believe me ask Romina because she saw it, too. . . ."

What Romina said: "I left the classroom with Ndalu, more or less behind Isabel, except I don't know how we didn't see Bruno, but I remember that laugh really well. Excuse me, Bruno, but since we're all telling the truth here, I think you laughed because you were afraid, or at least you were nervous. Come on, admit it. There's nothing wrong with that; it was Empty Crate itself coming to our school. . . . The truth is that in the middle of the dust we were running towards that hole in the corner of the school wall when Comrade Teacher-Rocket passed us. It's not easy to explain. We talked about it yesterday. You had to be there. Her running combined the speed of a leopard with the jumping of a gazelle. It all happened so quickly that when we jumped the wall, the comrade teacher wasn't there any more. . . . We crossed the avenue there, went to the Party office, still running, and we only stopped at the National Radio station, but since we had our backpacks we decided it was better not to come back here."

After that the conversation became more jumbled. Nobody respected anyone else's turn to talk, everybody was speaking at the same time and we each wanted to improve some detail in our own version.

I was a little disillusioned because in the final analysis none of us had seen the truck, or even a man dressed in black, or at the very least heard a single shot, or, at the absolute very least, found some trace (I learned that word on TV) today such as a bloodstain or the shell of a bullet. Nothing. Nothing.

How annoying! I thought. I couldn't find out anything. I was going to return to my street with nothing to talk about. Some people would say that the whole thing had been made up, that Empty Crate hadn't even been at my school. But I was still suspicious: why was Murtala pissed off, and why did he have a bandage on his ankle? Why was the comrade English teacher walking so slowly today? Why hadn't the comrade chemistry teacher told us anything today, and why did he have such a funny smile? And why – this was the really annoying part – had only people who hadn't seen anything come to the meeting? Even stupid Luaia had the courtesy to faint, which meant that the foolish girl didn't even know if she'd been raped.

The group broke up, of course. There was nothing more to do. Cláudio was picked up in a military jeep and Petra took the opportunity to get a lift. Luaia went to the classroom to see if she could find the hairpins she'd been offered as a birthday present on the very day of Empty Crate, Bruno rushed home because he was already late for lunch, and Romina told him not to run or his mother would get angry.

"Are you sad?" Romina asked, as we were crossing the avenue.

"No . . ."

"But that look on your face. . . ." Her voice was sweet.

"You know I don't like goodbyes. . . . Today we were in May 1st Square and after the rally I started thinking. . . ."

"Thinking about what?"

"That things always end, Ró."

"But what are you talking about?"

"About everything. . . . For example, that happiness, with the shouting and the anthem and the slogans – it all ends, eh, people go home, they drift apart . . ."

"Don't be like that."

"No. . . . It's not that. . . . Look, we still have some classes left, then the final exams, then everybody goes on holiday, then there are people who don't come back or they change classes. It's always like that, Ró. People end up drifting apart. . . ."

"Are you talking like that because of Bruno?" It turned out that she knew.

"You already knew that he's going to Portugal?"

"Yes . . . But is that why you're sad?"

"It's not just that, Ró. That's just the beginning. . . . Every year people leave our classes. It's normal, but I can't get used to it. . . ."

"I know what you mean. When we go away on vacation I get this weird feeling. . . ."

"It's just. . . . You spend the whole year fighting off the teachers, waiting for holidays, but the holidays are what change people. Some of them don't come back, the jokes are never the same, but that's not the worst of it, Ró. . . ."

"What's the worst of it?" she said in her sweet voice.

"When we change schools, later on, or when we finish high school, then we'll never see each other again, we'll never have the same classmates. . . ."

"But there are always other classmates."

"No, Romina, 'other' classmates don't exist. . . . You know very well what I'm talking about. Our class, even with people moving in and out, is 'our' class. You know who I'm talking about. . . . And this class is about to end, don't you feel that?" I didn't want to look her in the eyes. I was afraid.

"Are you sad?" She seemed to be unsure whether to give me a hug.

"I don't know. . . . You know, when the goodbyes start they never stop again, they never stop. . . ."

"But what are you talking about?"

"Nothing, nothing. . . . You know what my grandmother says, Ró?"

"No, what does she say?"

"That we never realize when we're living the best days of our lives. . . ." This time I looked at her. "But I figure that's how it is. . . ."

"So?"

"I know these are the best days of our lives, Romina. . . . This running around, all the talk in the schoolyard, even if everybody exaggerates like crazy." I smiled.

"But more things are always going to happen to us, eh?" She looked at her watch.

"Yes, of course, more things are going to happen. . . ." I looked at her.

"But you're sad? Right?"

"A little, Ró, a little. . . ."

We said "bye," each heading towards our own house. It was here that I was going to say that at times all the big things in life can be seen in one small thing. You don't have to explain much: it's enough to look.

The end of the school year was always painful for me because I missed my classmates, our jokes, even the comrade teachers, even the slogans, even singing the anthem, even going to write on the board, even the general cleaning of the school, even playing statues in the corridor with your hands above your head until your back was burning, or inventing insults to yell at each other until the comrade deputy principal caught us and gave us all two strokes of the ruler on each hand – all that stuff, it was all just one life, which one of these days was going to end.

These days, when I couldn't stop myself from thinking about these things, I became sad because, even though there were still many years left before the end of my school days, one day they were going to end, and elders don't act up in the classroom, they don't get detention points, they don't talk nonsense to Cuban teachers who don't understand nonsense. Elders don't naturally exaggerate the stories that they tell, elders don't take forever to talk about what somebody did or would like to do. Elders don't know how to invent a good put-down!

This business of being old must be a ton of work.

II

"Oh nostalgic sadness, oh beloved companion
Reinvigorating my senses
You sweeten my whole existence."

—Óscar Ribas, *Cultuando as Musas*

here in Angola there's no doubt that something's
going to happen. . . .

It was night, and Aunt Dada and I were talking on the balcony. She was telling me how her holiday in Luanda had been: what she'd done, the places she'd visited while I was at school. She was leaving the next morning, and we hadn't spoken for a few days, so we were bringing each other up to date, although, of course, we weren't getting up to *day*t but up to *night*.

Yes, night has a smell.

At least here in Luanda, at my house, with this garden, night has a smell. I saw on television that there are some plants that open only at night. I call them bat-plants, and I don't know if there are bat-plants right here in this garden, but night brings other smells onto this balcony, that's for sure.

If what I'm going to say is true, then that night had a hot smell, which could be a thing where, if you think about it, you put very scarlet roses, bows of creepers with a pinch of dust, lots of grass, the sound of crickets, the sound of slugs ambling over spittle, the sound of grasshoppers, a single peep of cicadas, a small cactus, green buds, two large banana leaves and an enormous clump of verbena and squeeze them all together and out would come the smell of that night.

"It smells so good here," my aunt said.

"That's the bat-plants. . . ."

"Which plants are those?"

"They're plants that prefer to come out at night, like the bats . . ."

"Ah. . . ." She smelled the air. "And here there are also bat-mosquitoes. Those are the ones that like to bite you at night. . . ."

We laughed at her joke.

"Aunt . . ."

"Yes, dear?"

"Do you know why the mosquitoes bite so much?"

"No, dear. Why do they bite so much?"

"Because they're thirsty!" I glanced at her. "And do you know why they're thirsty?"

"Why?"

"Because, as you know, mosquitoes are born in puddles of water. . . ."

"Yes. . . . So?"

"Well, since they're born in the water, when they start flying they remember their home, that's to say, their first home, the water . . . So they bite us looking for water."

"And they don't find it."

"Yes, but if there's nothing better around, they drink blood," I explained in a serious voice.

"Who told you that, dear?"

"Nobody told me, Aunt, it's just what I know. . . ."

But in fact those mosquitoes were very thirsty and we decided to go inside. I had to go and tidy up my room. She went with me.

"Aunt, when are you coming back here?"

"I don't know, dear. I really don't know."

"Next time you come here can you bring your children with you so that we can get to know them?" I was rummaging in a box full of old workbooks.

"Yes, I could." She picked up one of the workbooks.

"That's an old workbook from my Portuguese Language class."

"Can I look at it?"

"Sure."

"Who's this Ngangula you're talking about here?"

"Ngangula, Aunt – it's Ngangula!"

"But who is Ngangula?"

It was incredible that she didn't know. "Oh, Aunt, don't tell me you don't even know who Ngangula is?!"

"I don't think I do know because you're not telling me. . . ."

"Look, I never thought that in Portugal they hadn't heard of Ngangula. . . . But you lived here in the old days. Don't you remember Ngangula? Weren't you ever told about him?"

"I don't think so, dear. Not that I remember."

"All right, then, first read this composition. It's about him. . . . Then you'll understand. . . ."

She started to read. I continued rummaging. It was a lot of work rummaging around in those old workbooks. I found hilarious compositions from grade two or three, with ridiculous kindergarten drawings, division tables – all things that now looked out of date.

"So this Ngangula is a hero . . ."

"Of course he is. He was tortured. They beat him a million times, kicked him a million times, but he didn't tell them where the guerrillas' encampment was. . . ."

"Hmmm. . . ."

"I find it weird that you don't know about Ngangula, Aunt. Everybody knows who he was. I bet that even in Cuba they know who he was. . . ."

"Well, I don't know, I never heard about him. . . . And he was very young, wasn't he?"

"Yeah, he was just a kid. . . ."

"And very brave."

"That's for sure. If it had been somebody from my class in this story by the second punch they would have told them the licence number of the president's car. Fortunately, I don't think the president's car has a licence plate. . . ."

We might have talked much longer, but Bruno Viola was downstairs. He told my sister that he had incredible news. I realized that, finally, after almost a week, we'd got a report from somebody who'd seen something.

This meant I had no choice: I had to go back out onto the balcony, among the bat-mosquitoes, because Bruno was sure to shoot his mouth off while telling the story, or else he'd have to shout while describing some scene, which would make it annoying to be there in the living room in front of the elders. I mean, this is what I was thinking. I went to open the front door for him.

"What's happenin'? You got news about Empty Crate, or what?"

"Warts and all. I've got the official version. I mean the complete version!" he said.

"I know what the official version is, Bruno. I hear it on the news every day."

"Hey, let's go sit down, buddy. You're gonna be stunned. . . ."

"Oh Bruno, lay off with all the suspense. Just spit it out!" I wanted to hear it now!

"Like this," he said, running his hand over his neck.

"Like what? You got a tickle in your throat?"

"I'm dry. You expect a guy to tell a story. . . ."

"Fuck, Bruno. You want a soft drink just for telling me the story?"

"Yo, you know how it is. The story goes down better. . . ." He swallowed his spittle slowly, to show off his thirst, the bastard.

"Okay, wait here. I'll see what I can get."

Of course what I was going to get was my supper-time soft drink, which would no longer be part of my supper. I put ice in the glasses and told my mother that we were going to sit out on the balcony and talk.

"I don't need a glass. I'll drink it out of the can," Bruno said.

"No! You'd drink it from the can if you were drinking it all yourself, but since we're going to share it we need glasses."

"Okay, pour it."

"Go on, start talking. . . ."

"Hey, you missed everything!"

"Yeah, I know I missed everything. And all my buddies missed everything, too, because we were the first to run."

"But you don't know what you missed, you wet-behind-the-ears."

"Your uncle's wet behind the ears. . . . Now tell me or I'm going to take your drink away," I threatened.

"You're not gonna believe me, but Empty Crate never came to the school."

"Empty Crate wasn't at the school? You kidding me, or what?"

So he had only come here to get my soft drink.

"It gets worse. There wasn't any crate or any truck or any shots or any raped women teachers or anything like that!"

"Oh, but . . . There were people who saw . . ."

"Saw, saw! . . . Saw what?"

"Hey, I don't know. . . . They were sure talking a lot. I figure they saw the truck arriving."

"No way! They didn't see a truck. They saw the dust, which came from a car. But it wasn't any Empty Crate truck."

I was stunned, as Bruno had said. So what had all that shouting been about, who had seen the truck coming, why had the entire school started to yell and run, and, above all, how had they struck such fear into the comrade English teacher as to make her run in that supersonic style?

"Hey, I was told this by a guy in Room 3 who couldn't run because he got stuck at his desk, so he saw everything . . ."

"What did he see?"

"It was like this: the whole school started to run because everybody was shouting, so everybody thought that somebody had actually seen Empty Crate arriving, and nobody waited around to see if it was really true."

"Yes . . ."

"Right, so then everybody started to run and jump over the walls. Well, this guy was on the floor and putting his head up to take a look. I don't know how his head didn't get trampled. Of course he's got this ridge on the nape of his neck that makes people respect the size of his head. . . ."

"Yes, Bruno. Get back to the main event, you're starting to exaggerate. . . ."

"Me? Exaggerate? Fuck, don't you even trust me? Then listen to this: when a lot of people had already split, the school was quiet, very quiet, with just one person crying in our room. . . ."

"It must have been Luaia," I interrupted.

"Sure, it must have been her. . . . Because this dude also saw the comrade chemistry teacher go to the teachers' offices and say that he was going to resist, that we were a bunch of cowards, that you had to fight back, and I don't know what else. . . ."

"Yes, go on." I scratched my legs. The mosquitoes were eating me alive.

"And he thought it was all over when he heard a car arrive . . ."

"Whoah! And it was Empty Crate?"

"No . . . You're not gonna believe . . ."

"Who was it? Tell me, Bruno!"

"It was the comrade inspector!!!"

We let rip with a howl that frightened even the mosquitoes. The poor comrade principal – what an embarrassment! So much preparation for the surprise visit, the school as neat as a pin, everybody in position, as they like to say, and when the comrade inspector arrived, the whole school ran away. I threw myself on the floor so I could laugh harder.

"But wait, that's not all," Bruno said.

"Go ahead. . . ."

"When the comrade inspector asked if there was anybody there, or clapped his hands or whatever, the chemistry teacher came out with a crowbar in his hands and said, 'Death to the *bandidos*! Bring on those bastards. *Víctoria o muerte*!' and I don't know what else, but fortunately he tripped and fell before he was able to crack the comrade inspector's head . . ."

"Ahahahahahahaha." I couldn't stop laughing because, aside from the humour of the situation, I could see the whole scene in my head.

"Calm down, I haven't finished," Bruno said.

"Fuck, Bruno, you deserved a whole soft drink just to yourself."

"Hey, if you want to look for one . . ."

"I can't. There aren't any left."

"Then let me finish: before the chemistry teacher could get up, the comrade inspector ran for his car and took off. . . . Meanwhile, the comrade principal, who had seen his car from up in her office, came running downstairs, and she went running after the comrade inspector's car, which never stopped, of course, because he was afraid of getting that crowbar in the head. . . ."

"Hold it, Bruno: sorry, but your friend who was there on the floor, stuck under his desk – he saw all that?"

"Hey, I'm telling you, he had a good angle of vision . . ."

"And what else did he see?"

"Hey, I figure all he saw was the comrade principal bawling out the Cuban teacher, and asking why the students had run away, and what all the shouting was about."

"And what did he say?"

"He said . . ." Bruno started to laugh. ". . . He asked the comrade principal how it was possible that she was acquainted with this Empty Crate when everybody else was afraid of him. . . ."

"Ahahahahahahaha." I laughed like crazy.

"Which means that the poor beggar hadn't understood anything about anything. You see, he still thought that the comrade principal was a buddy of the comrade inspector, who had been promoted to Comrade Empty Crate. . . . Ahahahahahahaha."

Bruno Viola laughed so hard that he almost fell off his chair.

"But Bruno, then what about the story that Eunice told me the day before?"

"What story?"

"Well, wasn't she crying at the front door and saying that Empty Crate had surrounded Ngola Kanini School?"

"Ha! She sure fooled you guys. . . ."

"Why do you say that?"

"She was with her sweetie, they had a fight or something, and to stop my mother from asking questions, she told this story about Empty Crate."

"Ah, now I understand."

Whether or not all of that was true, it was more or less the real version of events because Cláudio also phoned me that night, and he'd heard a very similar version, except that it included Luaia being dragged out of the classroom by the comrade chemistry teacher, who hauled Luaia by the neck to Comrade Teacher Sara's room, which, in fact, was more or less what Luaia had told us. It was Cláudio, too, who explained Murtala's bad mood to me: the truth is that, in the midst of the rush, Murtala fell once, but managed to stand up before being knocked down by the others, except that when he was about to jump over the wall, he fell very badly again, and this time he seriously injured his ankle. Even in the middle of that rush, tons of people saw him fall, and they all started shouting, "Baaad, baaad, baaad!" In other words, they were making fun of him, and even though nobody stopped to stick chewing gum on his face or take advantage of his vulnerable position, by the time he started limping away again he knew very well that each of those *bad*'s had been for him, which made his bad mood understandable, and on top of that helped to explain why he didn't even accept my water in case I also took advantage of him by subjecting him to some sort of delayed ridicule.

Exaggerated or not, things like this were possible in Luanda, even a whole school taking off in a rush, some of them almost being run over by cars, others being knocked over by people in the school yard, others fainting, and still others, or more precisely, one other, running lynx-style without touching the wall or leaving a mark in the dust. On top of that, all this happened on the same afternoon that a certain comrade inspector had decided – the loser – to make a visit; but who ordered his car to go so fast and churn up so much dust that everyone would think it was Empty Crate?

Wow! Here in Luanda there's no doubting good stories. Lots of things can happen and there are a lot of other things which, if they can't happen, can find another way to take place.

Fuck, here in Angola there's no doubt that something's going to happen. . . .

> It all depends on *los hombres*, on their hearts, on the firmness with which they struggle for their ideals, the simplicity with which they act, the respect they feel for their *compañeros*. . . .

As it happens, that morning I didn't wake up feeling great, even though it was the day to take Aunt Dada to the airport. I don't like this business of goodbyes at all.

We had breakfast early because it was necessary to "do the cheque-king," as my uncle used to say. I warned Aunt Dada right away to eat well because sometimes the wait to board the plane took longer than the trip to Portugal.

"You must be mistaken, dear, because the trip takes eight hours," she smiled.

"I'm not mistaken, Aunt. Just don't say later that I didn't warn you, okay?"

I knew what I was talking about. We carried in the luggage and the "cheque-king" alone took three hours: examination of the bags here, quarrel over the weight allowance there, questions somewhere else, passport control on the other side – all the usual stuff. The flight was scheduled to leave at noon, but I remember that it was ten o'clock at night when she boarded the plane, and the flight took off at eleven. A few days later I talked to her on the phone.

"You don't joke with Angolan Airlines, do you?" And she laughed.

That same afternoon Romina fulfilled the promise she had made concerning the famous snack. It was a marvel, brimming with delicious desserts and complicated names, from the abundance of soft drinks, the chocolate mousse, the banana cake, to large quantities of toasted almond paste, even though I only managed to attack three saucers. Murtala didn't come, I don't know whether out of shame at having vomited the last time, or out of shame at his fall, for which we still hadn't teased him as he deserved. But Comrade Teachers Ángel and María were there, and Cláudio, Petra, Luaia, Kalí, Bruno and I. The mood was good, although I have to say that the whiff of goodbyes lingered in the air. . . .

They put on a video, and Ró's mother, who is very considerate, brought two saucers of strawberry compote, one for each of the comrade teachers. You should have seen those faces: they stared at the sweets and they laughed, they ate a spoonful, they sucked the sweet in their mouths, they paused, they looked at each other, man and wife, smiling because of some strawberry jam. I thought it was a beautiful scene, but I couldn't say this to anyone, or else they'd make fun of me.

The film was about war. From this starting point Comrade Teacher Ángel began to talk about the Americans: they always won in the movies, but in real life they had to eat lots of shit, too. We started to say that in American films, the lead actor was always the best: his machine gun never ran out of ammunition; it wasn't like an AK-47 that only had thirty rounds. One time Cláudio and I counted. The dude in the film fired for two and a half minutes without a break and he still had a bullet left over to shoot down a grenade that was going to blow up the bridge. Yeah, that dude was an ace.

When the film ended, it happened: I'd scented that goodbye smell; why is it that goodbyes have a smell? You know, don't you? As soon as the film ended, Comrade Teacher Ángel almost succeeded in refusing the saucers of jam that Ró's mother offered him because he said he wanted to say a few things, but finally he decided to eat the fruit first and talk afterwards. In fact, he didn't want to say a few things, he wanted to say a number of them.

"*Bueno*," he said, "it's not easy to say what I have to say now. Above all, I don't want to ruin the good mood in this room now. But you are, up to a point, not just our students – my students and the students of *Camarada* Teacher María – but you're also our *grandes amigos*. And that's why *Camarada* Teacher María and I decided we were gonna give you the news today, more privately here, and not *mañana* when the whole school's gonna find out."

(Romina looked at me. At that moment she, too, sensed the smell.)

"You are young, but you must already know that lots of things have changed in your country recently. . . . The attempts to get a peace agreement, the so-called international pressure. All this doesn't just happen on TV, it's gonna happen for real in your country, in your lives, in your friendships. . . . Your country's changing direction and, as always, this has consequences. *La revolución*, as Che Guevara said, has many phases, some are easy and others are very difficult. Well . . ." He coughed. "Well, what I have to tell you is that in a very little time, I, *Camarada* Teacher María, the *camarada* chemistry teacher and many other Cubans who are here, are going back to Cuba."

(Everyone was shocked. Some people even stopped chewing.)

"This way, to make it less difficult, we decided to tell you this today. Also because here we are in a private situation where we can talk about your doubts, about why all this is happening. Above all, we wanted to tell you – you who are just Angolan children, you who are children in a school, and you who are our *amigos* – that the struggle, *la revolución*, never ends. Education is a battle. Your choice of training, if you decide to be teachers, mechanics, doctors, workers, peasants. . . . that choice is also a battle, a decision that changes the direction of your country. You, in fact, are a group with influence like others in your class. You're intelligent children, with a good education, your spirit is *revolucionario*. We've seen you work for the collective good, giving an explanation in class to a *compañero*, helping a teacher check homework. . . ."

(We were horrified. . . . Our spirit was *revolucionario*? I didn't even like to wake up early, and we all cheated on almost all our exams. . . .)

"The good that you do to another person, the good that you do for your country, for society, it is in your hearts, it comes from there." (Petra started to cry.) "In addition to feeling that we've completed our mission in Angola, in addition to feeling privileged to be able to help our Angolan brothers, we're returning to our *patria* happy to know that Angola has young people who, in their majority, are so dedicated to *la causa revolucionaria* because *la causa revolucionaria*, before anything else, is progress. Angola's taking the first steps in another direction, but it could be the right direction. It all depends on *los hombres*, on their hearts, on the firmness with which they struggle for their ideals, the simplicity with which they act, the respect they feel for their *compañeros*. . . . Angola is already a great nation, and it is gonna grow more! Remember Che Guevara: even when he was a man of international reknown, he continued to volunteer in the factory." He paused. "Simplicity is a value to hold onto. The *hombre* of tomorrow, the *hombre* of progress does not tremble before the attacks of *imperialismo*. He does not back down before the will of those who think the world belongs to them, he does not dirty himself in the mud of corruption – all in all, the *hombre* of progress does not fail!"

(Even Ró's mother looked impressed. Cláudio yawned.)

"*Bueno*, to conclude, I wanna wish you happiness and tell you from the heart – my heart as much as that of Teacher María – that you were a marvellous class. . . . and that children really are the flower of humanity. Never forget that . . ."

And, well, it turned out that Comrade Teacher Ángel also had a tear to wipe away from the corner of his eye. We applauded; Comrade Teacher María and Petra cried openly, I don't know about Ró – I couldn't see her face – and I'd become a little emotional myself but I couldn't show it because Cláudio was watching.

Ró's mother said it was best to wash down those words with a toast, and brought a bottle of champagne.

Then something occurred that happens to me once in a while. I started to see everything in slow motion, as if it were a black-and-white film: the glasses clinking, the smiles on everyone's mouths, Petra's reddened eyes, and, finally, the toast!

Sentences mingled in my head: a toast to all the departing Cubans, a toast to mark the end of our contact with the Cuban comrades, a toast to the end of the fraternal collaboration between the Cuban people and our people, a toast as well to the end of the school year, a toast, also now, to Bruno, who was leaving, a toast to the fact that we didn't know who would still be in our class next year, a toast because we don't know if anyone is going to write to those Cuban teachers, a toast in order that when they return to Cuba, as a result of their time in Angola, they may have better living conditions: maybe more meat every week, maybe a car, maybe a little more money, maybe. . . . And now a toast to the heartfelt words of Comrade Teacher Ángel, a toast to Comrade Teacher María's tears, a toast to the pride she felt as she saw her husband speak, a toast to the boys in this class who also felt like crying, a toast to Cuba, please, a toast to Cuba, a toast to the Cuban soldiers who fell on Angolan soil, a toast to the good will, the sacrifice, the simplicity of these people, a toast to Comrade Che Guevara, a significant man and an insignificant worker, a toast to the comrade Cuban doctors, a toast to us as well, the children, the "flowers of humanity," as Comrade Teacher Ángel called us, a toast to the future of Angola and its new direction, a toast to the man of tomorrow, and, of course – how could we forget this, Cláudio? – a toast to Progress!

Ró's mother asked Comrade Teacher María if she wanted to say a few words, and even though she didn't say yes, everyone was afraid that her few words might turn into the many words of her husband; she always spoke much more quickly and with a greater number of words than he. But she refused. She asked only that we pass her a handkerchief, "No, two handkerchiefs, *por favor,*" because the snot was already rolling from her very fat nostrils.

We didn't stay very late at Ró's house. Final exams started the next day; some people still wanted to go home and review the material, others wanted to look at the material for the first time, others just wanted to go home with the Tupperware containers that Ró's mother was certain to provide. Someone even asked: "Dona Angélica, do we need a ration card here to have cake?" And the gang laughed, but that only made me wonder whether, with all the changes, ration cards, too, were going to disappear.

Up above, in the window, Teacher Ángel had his hand on Teacher María's shoulder, and was kissing her on the cheek to stop her from crying so much.

I wasn't going to be able to have milk in my breakfast coffee, as I usually did in the morning, because, since I was nervous about the first day of exams, coffee with milk would make me colicky. On these days I drank tea. I liked having to go out into the garden to pull up fresh verbena, although some people prefer to dry it first. The leaf is a bit rough, with tiny little nicks in the side, and it takes care, but it's only if you pull too hard on it that you're going to cut yourself. Before getting close you're hit right away with the smell of the verbena cluster, which, if the garden has already been watered, is wonderful.

I heard the sound of boiling tea, but I let it be. It had to keep boiling for a moment.

"Dad, can you drive me to school today? So I don't get there late?"

"Yes, son."

"Hey, great."

He was just being kind. I wasn't late, but everybody liked to get a lift on exam days. I don't know why. Maybe we needed to feel a little different on those days, so we went by car.

But, as we were finishing breakfast. . . .

"Good morning, son."

"Oh? Good morning, Comrade António. Are you here? It's so early. I didn't even hear you come in."

"I have the key, son."

"And why did you come so early today?"

"Don't you have a test today, son?" He was laughing.

"Yeah, exams start today."

"So I came to wish you good luck, son!" He started to pick up the used cups.

"Thank you, António. . . . And leave that there. I'll take everything into the kitchen."

But he was stubborn, stubborn. As there weren't many items on the table, he took only a few each time to increase the number of trips. He opened the kitchen windows, shooed away the cat, which was sleeping next to the door, went to turn on the gas, opened the larder and began to sweep the back yard.

"What's for lunch today, son?"

"I don't know, António. My mother's still upstairs."

"I'm going to take out fish!" He walked towards the larder.

"António, don't take anything out yet. It's better to find out if anybody's going to be here for lunch."

"Who? Your grandmother?"

"I don't know, António, I don't know."

While my father went upstairs to get ready, I sat down in the yard. I couldn't see the avocado tree from there, but I could hear its leaves, smell its strong scent, hear an avocado fall. "Mine!" I shouted, even though neither of my sisters was there to dispute the avocado with me. I went to put the avocado on the shelf in the larder.

"Comrade António, can you do me a favour? . . ."

"Tell me, son."

"When my sisters wake up . . ."

"Yes."

"Just tell them that this avocado here is already taken, okay?"

"I'll tell them, son."

Just in case, I went to look for a knife and carved my initial into the avocado. But this was mere "protocol," as we said. Maybe by lunch time there would be two or three more avocados, but this was a childhood habit. When a mango fell, we said, "Mine!" When the doorbell rang, we said, "I'm not going, I called it." When we were getting into the car, we said, "I'm in front. I called it!" If there was only one mango, we said, "The stone's mine!" If we found a coin, we'd grab it, saying, "Finders keepers!" When someone got up, leaving a chair empty, we said, "When the cat's away the mouse will play!" We heard an elder say, "Who wants . . . ?" and we immediately said, "Me!" A fig fell to the ground and we would say, "The seed's mine!" – all of this in a state approaching military alert, all of it totally automatic.

"What test do you have today, son?"

"Portuguese Language."

"Hmm. . . ."

"Comrade António . . ."

"Yes, son."

"You've heard that all the Cubans are going away?"

"I think I heard that, son."

"Everything's going to change, Comrade António. . . . Don't you think so?"

"It looks like peace is coming, son. . . . That's what they were sayin' in my neighbourhood yesterday."

"They were talkin' about that? About peace?"

"Hmm . . . Looks like we're gonna have peace. . . ."

"Do you really believe that, António? . . . How many years have we been hearing that guff?"

"It could happen, son, it could happen. . . ."

He came out of the larder with an enormous fish.

"Do you know who caught that fish?" I grabbed my backpack and put it on.

"It was your father," he said.

"No way. It was me," I said, trying it on.

"Hmm . . . Son, are you catching such big fish already?" He started to laugh.

I didn't reply. What could I say? I looked at the fish, calculating its weight. Not even with a great story invented in my sharp morning mind could I fool Comrade António.

"See you tomorrow, Comrade António . . ."

"See you later, son. . . . See you later . . ."

I arrived at school by car; Cláudio too; even Bruno's mother brought him to school that day. It was required that you bring your identity papers on the day of a test, but some people's I.D.'s had expired, others had forgotten, others brought their birth certificates. There were always *makas* as we were going into the classroom and the tests started half an hour late.

Even during tests two of us sat at each desk; there was no other way to fit everybody in. The teachers were more vigilant than usual, but by the middle of the test we could see some of what the person next to us had written, and by the end we were even able to ask each other questions as long as we did it in a very low voice.

It worked more or less like this:

> if the teacher was very alert, the student pretended to be thinking and rested his head on his hand; from this position he could let his gaze slide sideways, but he had to be careful not to turn his head or else the teacher would pick up on it right away;
>
> if the teacher was gullible, you could drop your eraser on the floor at the same time as the person across the aisle from you; then you asked, "Comrade Teacher, can I pick up my eraser?" When the teacher said, "Yes," the two students exchanged erasers, taking advantage of the moment to exchange, at the absolute maximum, three words (but you could also write numbers or short phrases on the erasers);
>
> if the teacher was reading during the test, the "normal" students would talk together, exchange ideas and show each other their answers; the "brave" students would pull cheat sheets out of their pockets or read words written on their arms, hands or legs, not to

> mention their bellies and chests; the "daring" students opened their backpacks and took out their notes, or talked with classmates who were sitting far away, going to the point of handing each other their tests for a few minutes.

Our group usually got good marks because everybody studied for the end-of-semester tests, so that conversation was limited to cases where we had doubts. The person who sat in the middle of the room had to be really good at the subject in order to sit in a spot where everybody could talk to him. Even in this regard, the comrade Cuban teachers were kind because when they caught someone cheating they only gave them a warning; they didn't confiscate the person's test.

That dumb Murtala, one day he was sitting there with a cheat sheet right on top of his desk when the comrade coordinator of physics came into the room and looked at him. But I don't think she saw anything. He looked so guilty that she asked: "What's wrong? Are you feeling all right?" As she walked towards him, Murtala barely had time to swallow his cheat sheet, almost without chewing. I think it was two whole pages. Of course after that he had to leave the room to vomit.

"Fuck, that dude's always puking!!!" Cláudio said, and we all laughed.

The test had gone well, really well: that was what I told my mother when I got home, starving to death, at twelve-thirty. I arrived happy and soaking wet. One of those half-hour showers that looks like it's not going to happen then happens had fallen, and the city was almost drowning because some of the storm sewers had backed up and the streets looked like rivers, and the poor neighbourhoods almost floated away. But I'd walked home slowly: it had been so long since I'd been caught in the rain.

At home, I found one of my grandmothers, a girl cousin, everybody from my house and Papí, which was a real surprise. Papí usually only appeared in the evening, when he could ring the bell and stand chatting with my sister at the front gate, even though everyone knew (and he knew himself) that he didn't have a chance with her.

"Papí," I greeted him. "You came early today."

"Hey, but your mother gave me a real talking-to! . . ."

"Why'd she give you a talking-to?"

"Well . . ." He had a towel in his hand and was rubbing his face and his hair. "So, so much rain that I just felt like sliding on your balcony. . . ."

That much was true. Papí had this habit: one other time when it was raining, he'd laid his hands on a hosepipe, doused down the balcony and was about to start sliding when my mother caught him. Maybe he had come now to get his revenge by sliding again.

"Your mother's so nice. . . ." He was laughing. He trembled.

"Why?"

"She only gave me a tiny little talking-to and then she invited me to stay for lunch."

I found this odd because Papí was a person who had a certain way of eating – I guess I can use this word – a categorical way of eating. Or, as my father said, "He doesn't waste time," and if there was one thing Papí didn't like to waste time doing, it was eating. With my grandmother and my cousin in the house, was my mother really going to invite him to have lunch with us?

"Yes, dear, but I asked Comrade António to make more food."

"It's your decision, Mum, but don't say later that I didn't warn you!"

To explain what Papí looked like, it would be necessary to imagine a huge ball, as if there were a soccer ball the size of a human being. To imagine how much he was capable of drinking I'd have to tell you that the young people in our neighbourhood held a potluck dinner with eighty people and at one-thirty in the morning, thanks to Papí, they ran out of soft drinks. But for you to really know who Papí was, I have to tell you that everybody liked him, that he liked everybody and that he was a really friendly guy.

"Make yourself at home, Papí, serve yourself," my mother said.

I swear on the soul of my grandfather, may he rest in peace, so that nobody says that I'm exaggerating: Papí served himself seven times in a row without a break, he gobbled down twenty-four slices of breaded beef, put thirty-two spoonfuls of white rice on his plate (my sisters counted them), drank two cans of Coca-Cola and, when my mother told him there wasn't any more, he managed to knock back a litre and a half of water. Grandmother Chica couldn't help saying: "After this, young man, you're going to the doctor to see if you have parasites!"

We all started giggling like crazy, since we'd been holding back our laughter for a long time. It was great.

"No, grandmother, that's the way it is!" Papí said, stroking his stomach. "It's just one of life's challenges . . ."

In the afternoon we went to the comrade Cuban teachers' house. They lived in those ridiculous buildings. Petra knew which building it was, in spite of their being all the same, because theirs had a painting of Comrade José Martí[7] over the door.

Ró's mother had provided three enormous strawberry compotes. We saw right away that they were going to love them.

"Come in, come in . . . Sit down, I'm gonna call Ángel," Teacher María said.

We sat down on chairs that were full of holes and started to look around: they had a black-and-white TV, the table only had three legs and the chair next to it was just like the ones at school.

"I'm gonna make tea for us," Teacher María said.

We were a little bit ashamed. I don't know why; they were our friends now. Maybe it was because we were at their house. Bruno

---

7 José Martí (1853-1895): Cuban poet, essayist and independence hero.

put his hand on his nose, as if the place smelled bad, but Petra responded by giving him a look that made him straighten up. I didn't say anything, but I thought it smelled like mould, too.

"Good afternoon, *compañeros.*" Ángel started to shake hands and kiss the hands of the girls in a Don Juan style that made them embarrassed. "Forgive my lateness, I was packing things for the trip."

"Good afternoon, Comrade Teacher!" we replied.

Teacher María came out of the kitchen with her huge smile, carrying the water for the tea. Since there were a lot of us, some drank from glasses, some from cups and two people were going to have to drink from saucers, but Bruno said he didn't feel like tea. "Thank you very much."

But I wondered: was it really tea? I mean, is one tea bag divided by two glasses, four cups and a saucer still tea? Being the last, I had to imagine that the substance was sugar juice, then I realized that it wasn't necessary to imagine because it was sugar juice.

"How are your exams goin'?" Teacher María asked.

"Very well, really very well," Petra said with a smile.

"So, are you all gonna pass?"

"Yes, almost all." It was Petra again.

"Of course Mortala," – they always called him that – "has many *dificultades.* He doesn't have enough of a base to *pasar* the course. . . ."

I don't know if it was true, but Cláudio told me that when we did fractions again this year, Murtala said that the only fraction he knew was a fraction of a second but he didn't know how to write it. Later, in a composition, he wrote that adolescence was when girls "got their monstruation"; but the worst was when, in physics class, he said he agreed with the suggestion of the Comrade Samora Machel, President of Mozambique, that we should ride a spaceship to the sun. When he was told that this was impossible because the sun would burn up the ship and the people, he gave exactly the same reply as Comrade President Samora (according to what I was told): "Fucking idiots! We'll just go at night!"

In the middle of tea, Petra, with tears in her eyes, spoke to the comrade teachers and said: "We thank you, comrade teachers, for everything you've done for us. And also for everything that all the Cuban comrades have done for Angola, from the workers to the soldiers to the doctors and the teachers. Angola is grateful, and Angolans and Cubans will always be brothers . . ." Etc., etc., etc.

Cláudio whispered in my ear that Petra's mother must have written that, but I'm not sure: Petra wrote good essays, too. A moment later I was shocked. I don't know whether from emotion or for some other reason, but Cláudio decided to offer Comrade Teacher Ángel his watch. He'd put it in a package and everything, and Petra whispered in my other ear that his mother had made the package, and I thought so, too.

When Teacher María started to cry very hard, the rest of us were a bit lost. Bruno couldn't say goodbye to them, he just took off. Romina started to cry, too, and the strength with which Teacher María hugged us was amazing. I still hadn't managed to say anything, but when Comrade Teacher Ángel shook my hand and said, "The struggle continues!", this came out of my mouth:

"Comrade teacher. . . . I know that all that you said, comrade teacher, about the revolution is true and . . . the most important thing is that we be truthful . . ." And then I couldn't say anything else.

He hugged me and wiped away my tears. Then he hugged Romina. Then he hugged Cláudio. Then he hugged Petra. Then he hugged Kalí. Then he hugged Catarina.

"Tell Bruno . . ." Teacher María said through her thick tears, "that even though he lacks discipline, he's a good boy. . . ."

We left, and they came to the window to wave farewell. Bruno waved goodbye from down below; so did Romina, even though she was wiping her cheeks.

"Very good, Cláudio," Petra said. "I was very impressed by your gesture. . . . Congratulations!"

"Hmmm. You're gonna be really impressed by the new watch my dad's gonna give me on Friday!"

Bruno was walking in silence. I thought he was sad. He was the worst troublemaker in Comrade Teacher María's classes but, in spite of that, I always figured they liked each other.

"Are you sad, Bruno?" Romina seemed to enjoy asking the question.

"No. . . . Why?"

"You didn't even say goodbye to Teacher María." I approached him.

"Oh, didn't you guys notice?!" He started laughing.

"Notice what?"

"How was I supposed to kiss her on the cheek when she had tons of snot pouring out of her nose?"

The sky remained dark, ashen, as though night wished to come before its time.

Again we said goodbye.

Again that vision of each of us going our own way.

Up above, in the window, Teacher Ángel had his hand on Teacher María's shoulder, and was kissing her on the cheek to stop her from crying so much.

A solitary drop of rain fell on my head during that last time that we saw those comrade Cuban teachers.

> it was the water that brought that smell that rose from the earth after the rain, the water that made new things grow on earth.

The quality of light that I could see through the window of my room told me right away that it was going to be a grey morning. The studio art test was today and our classroom would be dark because the lamps were all broken. I just hoped that, if it started to rain, it didn't pour down onto my sketch pad.

We ate breakfast slowly. The exam started later that day because there was just the one, and it was the last one. The avocado tree stood almost motionless. I was afraid my father would say: "So? It isn't stretching itself today?" What could I say? Maybe the tree was still asleep, or maybe it felt cold, or perhaps the ashen sky had said something to the avocado tree that we didn't know how to hear, and that was why it was sad.

"Hell . . ." My father looked at his watch. "Comrade António's really on the hook today." This, in fishermen's jargon, meant that he'd slept in.

"Hmm. . . . I don't think so, Dad. He must be out there sitting in the garden. . . ."

The test went very well for me. The classroom was a bit dark and, in spite of the cloud-laden sky, the rain didn't fall. The studio art test was perfect for the final day because it allowed us to take advantage of all the leftover material – compasses, gouache, India ink, markers, felt-tipped pens, even plasticine – to make the last inscriptions of the year on the desks, the wall and the classroom door.

In the test we'd been asked to make a drawing of our choice, using certain prescribed techniques. We took advantage of the opportunity. It was striking; I'd noticed in all the studio art tests since grade four that everybody drew things that were connected to the war: three people had drawn AK-47s, two had drawn Soviet tanks, others Makarovs, and the girls drew things like women washing clothes in the river, or an aerial view of the Roque Santeiro Market, the Marginal at night or the hill where the fortress stood.

It was normal to draw weapons. Everybody had pistols at home, or even AK-47s, or if they didn't, they had an uncle who had one, or who was a soldier and showed them how the weapon worked. Cláudio even said one day that he knew how to assemble and dismantle a Makarov; his uncle had shown him how. But everybody thought this was a fib. Filomeno's drawing was very pretty. He'd even worked in the gleam that lingers after you've cleaned the AK-47's barrel, and at the side he'd drawn one of those magazines that looks like a double magazine and which the FAPLAs stand up back-to-back so that when they want to change magazines they just have to turn them around.

The subject of war, of weapons, arose, too, because everybody had already seen, and some had already fired, pistols. We talked heatedly at recess about this. There were people who'd heard bush-rumours about the battles in Kuando Kubango province, stories about how tough the South Africans were, but how they were scared shitless of the Cubans, *che*. When they heard that the Cubans were moving into an area, it was as if they'd seen a ghost. Everybody, elders or not, said that the Cubans were very good soldiers, brave, well organized, disciplined, good friends. The only problem was that they couldn't say Kifangondo[8], they always said: "Kifangondo-ete!"

---

8 Kifangondo: Site of a decisive battle, fought November 11, 1975, in which FAPLA soldiers, with Cuban support, defeated Holden Roberto's Western-backed FNLA (Angolan National Liberation Front).

War always appeared, too, in our compositions. Any student who was assigned a free composition would talk about the war; he would exaggerate; he would tell a story about his uncle, or he would say that his cousin was a commando, *che*, a tough guy, a ballbreaker, don't mess around with him. War appeared in our drawings (the AK-47s, the cannons we called "Monacaxito"), it came up in conversation ("It's true, I'm tellin' you! . . ."), it appeared on the murals (drawings in the army hospital), it was part of our put-downs ("Your uncle went to fight for UNITA, but he came back because he complained that his hair was full of lice . . ."), it appeared in public service announcements on TV ("Hey, Reagan – hands off Angola!"), and it even appeared in our dreams ("Shoot Murtala, fuck it, shoot!"). War even got into the mouths of crazy homeless people, like that nutcase who called himself Sonangol, after the oil company, because he always lathered himself with oil. You only had to look at his red mouth and his white eyes. He always said: "War's a sickness . . . Now I wanna know where yous are gonna get a pill for it . . . I'm warnin' yous, if yous catch war, every day you're gonna die a little bit, maybe it goes slow at first, but yous are gonna drop. . . . War's what makes a country itchy . . . Yous scratch and scratch and then the blood starts comin' out . . . War's when yous stop scratchin' but the blood keeps pourin'. . . ."

And he laughed, like that, with the oil running down his body. Petra said that maybe that oil running down him was his soul. What do I know.

I left the classroom, looked up at the sky. It was such an enormous place. The sky wasn't blue-een; it was more darkish, the colour of cement that's already a bit old.

"Don't you want to write your name?" Romina had come up to me.

"Eh?" I said, distracted.

"Aren't you going to write your name on the door?"

"Yeah, in a minute."

"You're already thinking about the farewells, eh?"

"No, actually I'm not."

"Hmm . . ." She looked at me.

"But it's the last time we're going to write on that door, that's true . . ."

We went over to where the others were. Some people were painting symbols on the classroom door; others were trying to draw their own faces. Filomeno was carefully drawing the Empty Crate car, the comrade principal at the entrance of the school and the students all shouting: "Welcome, Comrade Surprise-Inspector!"

From there we went to the area behind the classrooms, where it really stank of piss. We pulled all our books and notebooks out of our backpacks. I'd brought all my notes except the ones for Portuguese Language, which contained compositions that I liked. Cláudio took out his books; Helder and Bruno as well. We put them all together and lighted the fire.

Petra was terrified. There could be a *maka* if they caught us. But we made a point of lighting the fire right in the schoolyard. Bruno even joked: "The children around the fire. . . ."

The fire got bigger, the flames grew bolder, and we edged away.

"Hey," Murtala said. "Let the fire breathe!"

And the fire breathed, yes, free, yellow, absolutely enormous. That rush of heat felt really good; there was an unpleasant wind. On the other side of the flame, images looked like they were melting: I saw Bruno's face, his unkempt hair; I saw Romina's face, her curly hair; I saw Murtala's face, his eyes wide open.

"Well . . ." I looked at them. "I'm off."

"You're going already?" Cláudio said.

"Yeah, I'm splitting."

"I'm taking off, too," Bruno said.

Before we had time to say a word, Bruno picked up his backpack and put it on. He started away with his quick walk, restless. When Ró and I went to take a good look at him, he was already far away, next to the front gate.

"Brunoooo . . . ," I called. I waited to see if he was going to look.

"He's not going to look," Ró whispered to me.

He's going to look, I thought to myself.

Far away, next to the gate, Bruno lifted his hand and waved farewell. I never did see whether by moving his head just a little he was looking back or not. "Brunoooo. . . ."

"Till next year, Ró," I said.

"Till next year," she said.

"Ró. . . ."

"Yes."

"If you don't come back next year. . . . write to me and tell me where you are," I said.

"Fine." She looked at me, nodding her head with her eyes and with the curls in her hair. "Fine."

I went through Heroines' Square. I passed the National Radio station and stopped there, on the spot where, on the day of Empty Crate, Romina and I had stopped running. I remembered the comrade English teacher, her leaps, her speed, her technique for jumping over a wall without touching it. I passed Kalí's house and continued down the hill.

When I reached my house, the interior door of the front gate was open.

On the balcony, I saw my mother speaking to a woman with a black scarf on her head. I dragged my feet from the gate to the stairs: I opened the mailbox, where there was never any mail; I stood up two gas containers that were lying on their sides; I lifted a snail off the path and set it down in the grass; I cleaned my feet carefully on the mat before treading on the first step; all this just to catch a tiny little bit of their conversation. It was no use! They were speaking too quietly.

I greeted them with a, "Good afternoon," and then I saw the woman's face: it was Comrade António's wife. My mother waved me inside so I only had time to see that the woman's left hand was wrapped in a white cloth, and that my mother's eyes were very red.

The hall leading to the kitchen was full of silence: I didn't hear the pressure cooker, I didn't hear the comrade announcer speaking on Comrade António's radio, I didn't hear the noise of cups or cutlery, the table wasn't set, I didn't hear footsteps and, when I reached the kitchen, I saw no one. No one.

I realized immediately that Comrade António hadn't come. When he was absent someone from his house always came to let us know, but it was never his wife. It was always a son or daughter, and sometimes they came wearing a hat or a head scarf, but that scarf was never black. And when somebody came to warn that Comrade António couldn't come, in spite of having to whip up food for us on short notice, my mother didn't have bloodshot eyes.

I opened the kitchen door and sat down on the step.

I couldn't see the avocado tree from there, but I could hear the sound of the leaves shaking in the wind. The sky was very dark and if that wind was coming from the north, we were going to have a storm. My grandfather always used to say: "The worst wind comes from the north!"

"Let's eat. . . ."

My sisters had arrived.

The girls had moved quickly. They'd already set the table, and my older sister had even put together a tuna salad with canned peas and yesterday's Angolan black beans.

"Comrade António died this morning . . ."

But after that my mother couldn't say anything more.

It was very silent around the table, but out in the streets we heard shouting and gunshots fired in celebration. When we turned on the radio I finally understood: they were saying that the war was over, that the comrade president was going to have a meeting with Savimbi, that we weren't going to be a single-party state. They were even talking about elections.

I tried to ask: "But how can there be elections if in Angola there's only one party and one president –"

But they told me to be quiet and listen to the rest of the news. Then they told me to go to the kitchen to look for the oil, the vinegar and the red jindungo peppers. I tried hard not to cry. I pretended that Comrade António was there next to the stove.

"Comrade António, pass me the jindungo peppers, please. . . ." As he didn't reply, I said: "You see, António, now we're going to have elections here in Angola! I bet there weren't any elections when the Portuguese were here!"

But he didn't say a thing.

After lunch I went to lie down in the long green chair in the garden. It was a little windy, which was good because it meant I could doze off quickly to the sound of the rustling of the avocado tree's leaves.

On days when the sky wasn't so dark I liked to imitate the slugs in the garden and lie out in the sun. Over in the kitchen Comrade António made a lot of noise with the plates and glasses; it always took him forever to do the washing up. This was the sound to which I was used to dozing off. "Wake up, son. . . . It's bad for you to lie with your head in the sun. . . . Your mother's going to give you a talking-to," he liked to say.

"But has it really been so long, António? . . . I only slept a little bit," I'd reply.

"Hey, son! It's been more than twenty minutes. . . ."

I woke with the raindrops smacking my legs and cheeks. Suddenly a powerful downpour began to fall. I slipped under the roof of the shed and stayed there watching the rain. I thought immediately of Murtala: in his house only seven people could sleep at a time when it was raining; the other five had to stand up against the wall where there was a little jut of roofing that protected them. Later it was the others' turn to sleep. I swear that's how they did it; no more than seven each time. Each time it rained overnight, Murtala slept through the first three classes the next morning.

Looking at all that water, I remembered the compositions we wrote about the rain, the soil, the importance of water. A comrade teacher who was sure she was a poet used to say that it was the water that brought that smell that rose from the earth after the rain, the water that made new things grow in the earth. However, it also nourished the earth's roots; it made "a new cycle burst into life." In the end, what she meant was that, thanks to the water, new leaves sprang from the soil. Then I thought: "Hey. . . . What if it's raining all over Angola?" Then I smiled. I just smiled.

AFTERWORD

In May 2000, an African writer in his early twenties, who had published one book of poems, had a conversation with Jacques dos Santos, editorial director of the Angolan publishing house Chá de Caxinde. Dos Santos was seeking manuscripts for a potential series of books that would evoke themes related to Angola's tardy and troubled arrival at independence. He asked the young writer, Ondjaki, whether he had a manuscript that might fill the bill. "I didn't have anything," Ondjaki recalls. "But I lied and said yes. . . . He asked me when I could submit the manuscript to him and I told him in two months' time." At the time, Ondjaki was studying for a university degree in sociology in Lisbon, Portugal. In spite of his academic commitments, he completed his first novel in two months of concentrated activity. *Bom dia camaradas* was published in the original Portuguese in Angola in 2001, in Portugal in 2003 and in Brazil in 2006; it has been translated into French, German, Spanish, and now, as *Good Morning Comrades*, into English. Few novels offer such a sensitive, original and human account of the end of the Cold War as seen from an underdeveloped country.

For Ondjaki, *Good Morning Comrades* proved to be the first milestone in a prolific creative career. He continues to live in Luanda, writes fiction and poetry, and maintains his interest in theatre, filmmaking and visual art. Ondjaki's second novel, the magical realist fable *O Assobiador* (2002), has been published in English by Aflame Books in the United Kingdom as *The Whistler* (2008). His most innovative novel, *Quantas madrugadas tem a noite* (literally, "How Many Dawns Has the Night"), published in 2004, consolidated his literary reputation in the Portuguese-speaking world. Ondjaki's most recent book, *Os da minha rua*, ("The People from My Street"), published in 2007, marks a return to the urban

Luanda neighbourhoods of his childhood. The title echoes the title of *Nós, os do Makulusu* ("We, the People from the Makulusu District"), the seminal novel of the reclusive Angolan experimental writer, José Luandino Vieira, whose influence on Ondjaki's prose is at its most pronounced in *Quantas madrugadas tem a noite*.

If the characters and action in *Good Morning Comrades* feel vivid and immediate, it may be in part because most are drawn from life. Ondjaki, who already has nine books to his credit, admits that this is his most autobiographical work. "Everything in *Good Morning Comrades*, all of the people, all of the situations, come from life. The only part that isn't very true to life is the sequence of events." The author's rearrangement of his memories to create an artistic effect evokes the urban Angola of his adolescence: "I tried to bring to life the Luanda of the 1980s, which wasn't very present in literature. . . . I tried to speak of the Cuban presence here, which had not been worked through in Angolan fiction." Between 1975 and 1991, more than 400,000 Cubans served in Angola as soldiers, doctors and teachers. For Angolans of the generation of Ondjaki, and his narrator, Ndalu, born in the years following independence in 1975, Cubans were selfless, strange, naive, and known to be ferocious fighters. They were valued accomplices in bringing Angola to full nationhood after nearly five centuries of Portuguese colonialism.

Angola's colonial experience was among the world's longest. The first Portuguese explorers reached the southern part of the Congo region in 1482. Angola soon developed into a coveted source of slaves for Portugal's most prized colony, Brazil. Until the early 20th century, relatively few Europeans settled in the colony. Between the 16th and the late 19th centuries the slave trade, and most other business, was managed by the outward-looking commercial classes of the country's coastal areas. Dominant among this group were people known as Creoles: Africans, many of them with European surnames and some distant European ancestry as a result of marriage alliances made with Portuguese or Dutch traders, who had adopted a Catholic, Portuguese-speaking culture and, in most cases, no longer spoke African languages. In the late 19th century, as Portuguese immigration into Angola increased, the Portuguese government made its first efforts to separate the races in what had been a society of vigorous racial and cultural mixing. Under the fascist-influenced dictator António Salazar, who ruled Portugal from 1932 to 1968, a "New State" was implemented, which raised barriers between the races and accelerated Portuguese immigration into the colony. The New State's trampling of the Creole and *mestiço* (mixed race) middle and upper classes in order to create greater economic opportunities for poorly educated immigrants from rural Portugal, pushed tensions in the colony to breaking point. Protests were greeted with brutal oppression, and in 1961 guerrilla warfare broke out. By the time that Marcelo Caetano, Salazar's successor, was driven from office by a left-wing military coup in Portugal on April 25, 1974, three different guerrilla movements were fighting against the Portuguese government in Angola. None of these movements, however, succeeded in inflicting military defeat on the Portuguese army. In contrast to events in the Portuguese African colony of Guinea Bissau, for example, where independence was declared before the military coup in Lisbon, the guerrillas in Angola were denied the defining moment of a military victory over the colonizers. As a result, when the last Portuguese proconsul to Luanda slipped away under cover of night on November 10, 1975, the three insurgent groups were left to compete for power. The most politically conservative of the three movements, Holden Roberto's Angolan National Liberation Front (FNLA, in Portuguese), which received substantial support from Western powers by way of Zaire, was also the weakest in military terms, and was soon eliminated. The Marxist MPLA (People's Movement for the Liberation of Angola), whose support was strongest in the culturally Creolized coastal regions, extended its power from Luanda into much of the rest of the country. Jonas Savimbi, the unpredictable, often egomaniacal leader of UNITA (National Union for the Total Independence of Angola), enjoyed the support of the

Ovimbundu people of the central highlands, Angola's most numerous ethnic group. Savimbi's foreign alliances included, at different times, representatives of almost every known ideological tendency. Originally Maoist in orientation and backed by Beijing, the Swiss-educated, Chinese-trained Savimbi later became a proxy of apartheid South Africa, Ronald Reagan's White House and, in the post-Cold War era, of Ukrainian arms dealers and international diamond smugglers.

In 1975, when the MPLA declared Angola's independence, white-ruled South Africa responded by unleashing Africa's most potent army to invade Angola and overthrow the new government. As the South African invasion force approached the capital, Fidel Castro rushed to save his close friend, Angolan president Agostinho Neto, by dispatching troops to Angola. This personal initiative of Castro's, of which the Soviet Union was informed, but which, according to most reliable research, Moscow neither approved nor committed itself to support, proved decisive. A combined Cuban-Angolan army turned back the South Africans 200 kilometres from Luanda, eventually obliging the over-extended invasion force to retreat to Namibia. From this point on, the Cuban commitment to Angola grew. Cuban doctors and teachers flooded into the country, while the Cuban military became an essential part of the Angolan government's defence against UNITA and continued incursions by the South African military. Once established in Angola, Cuban commanders, such as Rafael Moracén, made decisions which put local interests ahead of promoting Moscow's Cold War agenda, often intervening in ways that marginalized politicians or military commanders who promoted closer coordination with the Soviet Union. Many Cubans saw themselves as sharing with Angolans a Creolized, Third World revolutionary culture; large numbers of Afro-Cubans traced their ancestry to the Angolan slave trade.

The Cubans' pivotal triumph occurred during the five-month battle of Cuito Cuanavale (November 1987-March 1988) when a South African-UNITA invasion was repelled by a combined Cuban-Angolan army. The last major battle of the Cold War, and the largest military engagement in the history of southern Africa, Cuito Cuanavale wreaked horrendous suffering on all sides. The number of soldiers who participated in this battle has been estimated variously at between 60,000 and 100,000 men. Fidel Castro personally directed the defence of the city in meticulous detail from his war-room in Havana. The failure of four successive South African assaults on Cuito Cuanavale, the defeat of the technologically superior South African military, the death of many white South African soldiers and the subsequent shooting down of South African Mirage jets by Cuban MiGs, changed the history of southern Africa forever. The battle of Cuito Cuanavale has been erased from history as it is taught in Western nations; yet this battle forced the Western world to accept Angola's present boundaries, caused the fall from power of South African president P.W. Botha, and led to the independence of Namibia and the end of apartheid in South Africa. In many parts of the world, Cuban soldiers, rather than tepid sanctions by Western nations, are credited with having dealt the apartheid system its death blow. But the battle of Cuito Cuanavale also set the stage for the end of the Cold War, and Cuba's eventual withdrawal from Africa.

This is the world inhabited by Ndalu and his friends in *Good Morning Comrades*: the world of a besieged Marxist regime whose physical integrity has been secured by the Cuban military in a war which, in spite of being geographically distant, remains present in the young people's imaginations. The Cubans are an inevitable presence; their departure, at the novel's close, foreshadows the disappearance of many familiar features of the pupils' daily lives: mass rallies, socialist holidays, school assignments on the worker-peasant alliance, and ration cards. The young people themselves are a cross-section of Angolan society typical of inner-city Luanda public schools of the 1980s. They belong to all racial groups, although, in an echo of MPLA multi-racialism, the students' races are never mentioned. There are Blacks, Creoles, *mestiços* (such as the author and his fictional alter-ego, Ndalu), East Indians and whites. The pupils at Ndalu's school also belong to all social classes. Many of these children are sufficiently well off to own watches or travel abroad; others, such as Murtala, live in houses so poor that the roof is not wide enough to protect the entire family when it rains. The integration of different levels of society is an important aspect of Luanda life of the 1980s recovered by the novel. Today, when many middle- and upper-class Angolans have moved out of the centre of Luanda to new suburbs south of the city, and more than 100 private primary schools offer elite tuition to those who can afford it, few Luanda schools would include among their pupils such a broad cross-section of society.

Young people of Ndalu's generation are both blessed and cursed. They live privileged lives by comparison with the violence experienced by rural Angolans, and they are able to lavish their adolescent energy on the idealistic early stages of a nationalist revolution. The petroleum-fed corruption that dominates contemporary Angola was less evident in the late 1980s; in a country at war, the absence of a democratic culture was a less pressing concern. But these young people are also cursed in being a generation that was destined not to complete secondary school together. *Good Morning Comrades* ends with the Cubans announcing their withdrawal from Angola and with plans for negotiations between the MPLA and Jonas Savimbi of UNITA. On June 14, 1991 the last Cubans left Angola. Around the globe, from El Salvador to Mozambique, local conflicts which had been exacerbated by the Cold War gave way to peace agreements and multi-party elections. Angola's tragedy is that its post-Cold War peace agreement failed. On September 29-30, 1992, elections convened by the United Nations gave two-thirds of the parliamentary seats to the MPLA; in the presidential election, Eduardo Dos Santos of the MPLA polled 49.5% and Jonas Savimbi of UNITA received 40.07%. An enraged Savimbi refused to accept the results. As David Birmingham writes, the United States "had promised him that if he stopped the war and went to the polls, he would undoubtedly win the election." Unfortunately, the United States had also assisted Savimbi in stockpiling weapons for his eventual ascension to the presidency. On November 12, Savimbi went back to war. Caught off guard, the MPLA reeled as Savimbi took over every other city in the country, then blasted his way into the outskirts of Luanda. Over the next decade, 300,000 people would die in an endless war of attrition. The fighting ended only in 2002, when Savimbi, who by this time had alienated nearly all of his international supporters, was tracked down and killed. The moment Savimbi died, UNITA dissolved as a military force.

In the mid-1990s, when Savimbi appeared poised to fulfill his promise to "drive the bastard children of the Portuguese Empire into the sea," Luanda parents who had the means to do so began sending their children out of the country to be educated. (Bruno Viola's departure for Portugal at the novel's close foreshadows this trend.) Classmates scattered and lost touch with each other. The Angolan reader, knowing the future that awaits the adolescents of *Good Morning Comrades*, is not surprised by the bittersweet nostalgia and "the smell of goodbyes" which descends on Ndalu in the novel's final pages. During his last extended conversation with his friend Romina, Ndalu says, "When the goodbyes start, they never stop again." This is both an insight into the nature of growing up – into adulthood as a succession of losses – and an almost morose foreshadowing of the fate of a generation destined to be scattered by the return of war to an Angola stripped of its Cuban protectors.

While Nelson Mandela and Ronald Reagan each receive passing mentions in *Good Morning Comrades*, the two poles of the children's understanding of the outside world are Cuba and Portugal.

Both Cuban teachers and residents of Portugal, such as Ndalu's Aunt Dada, who used to live in Angola when it was a Portuguese colony, misconstrue the realities of life in Luanda. The Cubans misunderstand the country because of their relentless revolutionary rhetoric. "I didn't even like to wake up early," Ndalu thinks in horror when Comrade Teacher Ángel proclaims the children's spirit to be *revolucionario*. The Portuguese misunderstand Angola because, like Aunt Dada, they cling to a colonial vision of Angolan history that excludes African heroes such as Ngangula; yet, in one of the novel's more critical threads, Aunt Dada also fails to grasp the nature of Angolan reality because, coming from a European democracy, she remains innocent of the harshness of life in an African dictatorship. The conflicting misapprehensions of local reality by Cubans and Portuguese enable the children to perceive what their country is not, and, by opposition, to begin to understand what it is and who they are. *Good Morning Comrades* recounts the coming of age of both a group of adolescents and a nation.

—Stephen Henighan

FURTHER READING

Patrick Chabal et. al., *A History of Postcolonial Lusophone Africa.* London: Hurst & Company, 2002.

Edward George, *The Cuban Intervention in Angola, 1965-1991: From Che Guevara to Cuito Cuanavale.* London: Frank Cass, 2005.

Ryszard Kapuściński, *Another Day of Life.* Translated by William R. Brand and Katarzyna Mroczkowska-Brand. New York: Harcourt Brace Johanovich, 1987.

Ondjaki, *The Whistler.* Translated by Richard Bartlett. Laverstock, U.K.: Aflame Books, 2008.

Pepetela, *Mayombe.* Translated by Michael Wolfers. London: Heinemann, 1996.

ACKNOWLEDGEMENTS

The publisher and translator thank the Instituto Português do Livro e da Biblioteca for support, and David Brookshaw for his careful critical reading of the translation. The translator thanks Ondjaki for his encouragement and willingness to be consulted, and Daniel Wells for his editorial guidance.

An excerpt from this translation appeared in *Words Without Borders*, September 2007.

ABOUT THE AUTHOR

Ondjaki was born in Angola in 1977. He studied sociology in Lisbon and attended film school in New York. He is the author of three novels and three short story collections, in addition to two collections of poems and a book for children. Ondjaki's novels and stories have been translated into English, French, Spanish, German and Italian. His novel *The Whistler* appeared in English from Aflame Books in the U.K. He lives in Luanda and has made a documentary film about his native city.

ABOUT THE TRANSLATOR

Stephen Henighan is the author of *A Grave in the Air*, *The Streets of Winter*, *North of Tourism*, *A Report on the Afterlife of Culture* and many other books. He teaches in the School of Languages and Literatures, University of Guelph, Ontario. (photo by Lorena Leija)